Peter and the Pilgrims

Books by Louise A. Vernon

Title	Subject
The Beggars' Bible	John Wycliffe
The Bible Smuggler	William Tyndale
Doctor in Rags	Paracelsus and Hutterites
A Heart Strangely Warmed	John Wesley
Ink on His Fingers	Johann Gutenberg
Key to the Prison	George Fox and Quakers
The King's Book	King James Version, Bible
The Man Who Laid the Egg	Erasmus
Night Preacher	Menno Simons
Peter and the Pilgrims	English Separatists, Pilgrims
The Secret Church	Anabaptists
Thunderstorm in Church	Martin Luther

Peter and the Pilgrims

Louise A. Vernon

Herald
Press

Scottdale, Pennsylvania
Waterloo, Ontario

Library of Congress Cataloging-in-Publication Data
Vernon, Louise A.
    Peter and the Pilgrims / Louise A. Vernon
      p. cm.
    Originally published: Washington, D.C. : Review and Herald Pub., 1963.
    Summary: When his kindly master dies, a ten-year-old orphan joins a
group of Separatists and follows them to Holland then to America, where
their quest for religious freedom becomes a struggle to survive.
      ISBN 0-8361-9226-5 (alk. paper)
        [1. Orphans—Fiction. 2. Puritans—Fiction. 3. Pilgrims (New Plymouth
Colony)—Fiction. 4. Christian life—Fiction. 5. Netherlands—History—
17th century—Fiction. 6. Massachusetts—History—New Plymouth,
1620-1691—Fiction.] I. Title

PZ7.V598 Pe 2002
[Fic]—dc21   2002027384

PETER AND THE PILGRIMS
Copyright © 1963 by Review and Herald Publishing, 2002 by Herald
Press, Scottdale, Pa. 15683
   Released simultaneously in Canada by Herald Press,
   Waterloo, Ont. N2L 6H7. All rights reserved
Library of Congress Catalog Card Number: 2002027384
International Standard Book Number: 0-8361-9226-5
Printed in the United States of America
Cover art by Allan Eitzen
Inside illustrations by Tom Dunbebin

12 11 10 09 08 07   10 9 8 7 6 5 4 3 2

To order or request information, please call 1-800-245-7894, or visit
www.heraldpress.com.

CONTENTS

THE MANOR HOUSE GHOST

The cook grumbled as she raked ashes from the kitchen fireplace.

"From tomorrow on, it's up at daybreak and to bed by midnight—if we're lucky. No telling how many guests the master will bring from London this time."

She straightened up with a grunt. "Well, would you look at that!"

She put her hands on her ample hips and stared at a small boy drowsing on a three-legged stool near the hearth. His straight dark hair hung in jagged peaks across his forehead. His face was long and narrow, with a determined chin. The upturned corners of his mouth gave him a saucy look.

"Wake up, Peter." The cook lifted a ring of iron keys hanging around her waist and jangled them over Peter's head.

Peter Cook twitched, blinked, and staggered to his feet. "Yes, ma'am."

"One more task for you, Peter Cook."

"Yes, ma'am."

"Off to bed with you." The cook's tone was not unkind. "I don't want master scolding me tomorrow for overworking his bound boy whom he treats like a son. My goose would be cooked for sure. I'm master's cook, and you're master's *Cook*. Unriddle me that, if you can."

The cook chuckled and shook a pudgy finger in Peter's face.

Peter was used to being teased, not only about his name, but about being an orphan boy, treated by the master like one of his own family.

The servants teased Peter because he always talked about the village of Scrooby, where his parents had lived. They sometimes hid his mother's Bible, his most precious possession, and made him hunt for it. They even teased Peter about his small hands and quickness. Peter did not mind.

"Here, take this." The cook thrust a lighted candle into Peter's hand and flapped her apron to shoo him out.

Peter stumbled across the stone floor and climbed the back stairs to his room in the servants' quarters. He made himself ready for bed, said his prayers, and blew out the candle.

An ear-splitting scream roused him from a sound sleep. He bounced up in bed, listening. Again and again the voice rang out in terror. Shivers ran up and down Peter's spine. As he listened, the cries died away into moans. An owl hooted, and Peter jumped out of bed. He heard excited voices in the hall and ran barefoot across the rush-covered floor.

9

Servants in nightgowns and nightcaps hurried ahead of him down the hall toward the portrait gallery. Their candles threw distorted shadows on the timbered walls.

"I saw it. I tell you I saw the Manor House ghost. Right here, under the master's own picture." The maidservant, huddled on the floor, pointed toward the portrait of the master of the Manor House. The master was dressed in green and gold velvet, with buckled sword. His light-colored hair curled to his shoulders and he held a plumed hat in his hand.

The maidservant picked at her dark, full skirt with nervous fingers. An empty candleholder lay in front of her.

"I was just coming up to bed, and as I walked up the main stairs to give things a once-over look, I felt something pass me. Like a wind, it was." She dabbed at her eyes with a corner of her apron. "Then it stood under the picture, all white and wavering. Those hollow eyes staring a hole right through me . . ."

Peter looked over his shoulder in spite of himself and edged closer to the cook.

"I couldn't move at first, and then it blew out my candle. And don't tell me it was the wind. There isn't any wind tonight."

The servants agreed and moved closer to one another.

"I can feel that cold breath yet. The cold breath of death, that's what it was." The maidservant rocked back and forth, her face in her hands. "Someone in this house is going to die."

The servants shuffled uneasily and stared at one another, their eyes wide.

Peter knew what death was. He had seen his mother die, but he had not been afraid, even in his grief, because she died with a loving faith in God. But ghosts and threats of death, something nameless and creeping, frightened him.

The manservant cleared his throat. "It's an omen, that's sure. Did you hear the horses neighing in their stalls tonight? Sounded as if they were crazy, they did."

The dairymaid nodded her head vigorously. "And the crickets have never left off chirping. That's an omen too." She kept on nodding as if she had forgotten how to stop.

"I heard an owl." Peter felt proud to add his bit.

The cook whirled around and clamped her big hand on his shoulder, almost lifting him off his feet. "Young man, what are you doing out of bed? You're far too young to hear things like this."

"I'm not either. I'm smart for my age. Master told me so. You can ask him tomorrow when he comes."

At this mention of the master the maidservant's sobs rose to a high pitch. "Tomorrow! Someone's going to die before tomorrow night. The Manor House ghost has never lied." She choked and sputtered through her sobs.

The cook gave Peter a shake. "Now see what you've done. To bed, all of you. There's a busy day ahead. None of us will sleep after all this." She nudged the maidservant down the hall like a mothering hen, with a warning glance at Peter to keep still.

When Peter hurried downstairs next morning he smelled bread baking. The servants still sat at the breakfast table as if they had all the time in the world.

"One thing I know. There were no ghosts around during the plague. Wasn't time. A person would be alive one minute and dead the next. They dropped like flies on the streets." The manservant wiped his mouth with the back of his hand.

11

The dairymaid was scornful. "People are stupid. The plague can be prevented. My mother sliced onions and put them all over the house to draw out the infection. We didn't get the plague."

The cook nodded. "My people used ginger brew—a teaspoon every day, every one of us, for three weeks. Awful tasting stuff but it worked."

She brought Peter a plate of eggs scrambled in butter and sent the servants flying to their work. "Out, out, all of you. Do you think we have all day to prepare for the master's coming?"

Peter's first task of the day was to scrape the loaves of bread free from oven grit and ashes. The cook made a great clatter as she reached into one stone niche after another for pots, jugs, and skillets to prepare the master's homecoming dinner. She put the roast on the cradle spit in the oven.

All the rest of the day Peter scurried from one task to another. The maidservant called him to help air the feather beds. They opened the windows and let the bedding hang out like giant tongues. Peter shook out the mats of woven rushes in the guestrooms.

"And mind, now, this afternoon you're to get fresh rushes for the servant's rooms," the maidservant instructed him. "It's been a month since they've been changed and the fleas are everywhere."

Peter helped the dairymaid store cheese and butter into crocks and vats, and went to turn the roast.

"All day long it's 'Peter do this, Peter do that,' " said Peter to himself when he began to tire. "I ought to sneak up the secret stairs and hide. They'd never find me."

When it was time to go to the river after rushes, Peter made sure that no one was looking and ran around the house to the main chimney. He had discovered a door there one day by accident when he was looking for a lost ball. A staircase led upward, but he had never dared to explore it before.

Peter pushed the door open with care, stepped inside, and closed the door until only a glimmer of light showed through. In almost pitch darkness he felt his way up a narrow stone stairway until he came to a solid wall. He pressed his hands over every inch of that wall. Near the floor he found a latch. A heavy door swung inward into a small room. One entire wall of the room was the chimney itself, now hot from the fire below. A slit in the outer wall permitted enough light for Peter to see.

There was still another door. Excited and fearful of being caught, Peter eased it open. He found himself in the hall near the portrait gallery. He heard footsteps, closed the door silently, and fled down the secret stairs into the open air. "I'll remember this," he chuckled to himself as he took the long way to the river. He passed through the backyard with its dovecote, chicken house, pigsty, and stable. At the river he cut a heap of rushes with the knife he always carried and started back with a heavy load in his arms. This time he came by the main road.

Peter was startled to see a sword and buckler in the road. "That looks like my master's sword," he said aloud.

As he started to pick up the sword, he noticed a plumed hat and a traveling cape a little farther on.

"Surely those are my master's hat and cape." The master was always fond of green and gold. Peter began to feel puzzled and frightened.

Just over the top of a grassy slope near the house, a man lay in the road, a man with light-colored hair. Peter dropped the rushes and ran toward him.

"It must be the master himself. No one else has hair like that. But it can't be—he's alone."

The man lay with his face in his arms. His legs were drawn up. His knee-length riding boots of fine leather were scuffed and torn. Peter knew those boots. He had helped the master into them many times.

"Sir—sir. Let me help you to the house." Peter bent down and brushed the long hair back. Then the master lifted his face. Peter cried out in horror. It was a face he knew and yet had never seen—swollen, almost black, like one open and running sore.

The master could hardly move his lips. "Black . . . plague."

Terror weakened Peter's knees. He sank down beside the master, trying not to look at his face.

"You can't stay here, sir. You must have help." Peter looked toward the house. No one was in sight. He propped the master into a sitting position.

"Help, help," he called. "The master is here. THE MASTER IS HERE."

Servants came running from every direction.

"Oh, who has done this terrible thing? The poor, poor man."

Peter, trembling from the weight, let the master sink back to the ground. The servants caught sight of his face, and their exclamations of pity turned into shrieks of terror.

"It's the plague—the black plague. It will kill us all."

Their faces were now distorted by fear. They shrank from Peter as if he too had the plague. The yeomen threw their aprons over their heads and darted into the house. The manservant slammed the front door and drove the bolt home. The servants shut and latched the windows. Peter ran to the other doors. All had been locked.

Peter looked at the master. He was lying very still—the stillness of death. Tears burned Peter's eyes. He choked, bit his lips, and clenched his fists. A blinding anger rose in him. He picked up a stone in each hand and beat at the front door. They would have to let him in.

The cook, holding a handkerchief to her face, opened a second-story window an inch or so.

"Go away, Peter. You can't come in. You would bring death to us all."

"But the master is dead. He must be buried."

The cook forgot to hold her handkerchief to her face as she began to wring her hands. "Lord, have mercy on us all. It's the waxen winding sheets and the death cart tonight."

Peter heard her call to the maidservant, "Here, take this key and unlock the chest in the downstairs hall. Take out the winding sheets."

The maidservant moaned and shrieked.

Peter cupped his hands over his mouth. "Unlock the door! I have no place to go, nothing to eat. How will I live?"

The cook ducked back inside, and Peter thought she was coming to unlock the door. Instead, she came back and tossed a loaf of bread at his feet.

"It doesn't matter where you go. Just never come back here."

The cook latched the window. Peter picked up the loaf of bread and brushed the dirt off. He looked up at the Manor House. Every door and window was locked and bolted against him. He could never enter the house again.

THE SECRET OF THE CELLAR

Peter waited until dark, so that no one from the house could see him. For the second time that day he climbed the secret stairs, this time in total darkness. He un-latched the door to the hall, listened for a moment, and felt his way to his room. He spread his cape on the bed and placed on it his mother's Bible, his clothes, and the loaf of bread. When he heard the servants at supper, he tiptoed to the dairy and took a round cheese with a hard rind. After wrapping everything in his cape, he went back to the secret room to sleep.

By dawn the next morning Peter was on the road to Scrooby, with his bundle of belongings tied to a short stick and carried over his shoulder. He had combed his hair, straightened his wide white collar, and adjusted the flared cuffs of his trousers neatly over his shoes. When the sun was high he put on his hat. About noon he came to a crossroads with no signs. No matter which way he looked he saw only rolling fields. He sat down by the roadside and cut himself a slice of bread and a slab of cheese, his first meal that day.

Far down the road a cart lumbered toward him. The carter wore short loose trousers and a sleeveless jerkin. A beehive-shaped hat almost hid his face as he dozed over the reins. The cart jolted over a deep rut and dislodged the carter's straw hat. Peter sprang to rescue it from the wheels.

"Oh, sir! Your hat! Here's your hat, sir."

"Eh? What's that? Oh, my hat." The carter stopped and rubbed a big red hand over his perspiring face. "Thank 'ee, thank 'ee, young'un." He pulled the hat low over his ears. "You be a long way from home, ben't you?"

"Yes, sir."

"You be a runaway?"

"No, sir."

"You be a schoolboy?"

"No, sir."

The carter took off his hat and scratched his grizzled head. "By your brave clothes, I see you're a gentleman's son."

Peter shook his head.

"Ay, don't try to fool me, lad. I know good cloth when I see it." The carter reached down and rubbed Peter's sleeve between big fingers. "Ben't you on a schoolboy vacation, perhaps? Tell the truth, now."

"I'm on my way to Scrooby to—to visit someone."

"Scrooby, eh? What do you know about that! I live in Scrooby myself. Yes, sirree. Climb up, climb up. I can take you all the way."

17

As they jolted down the road, the carter glanced at Peter's bundle. "How do I know you're not running away with the family jewels? He-he-he."

Peter opened his bundle. The carter pointed to Peter's Bible. "That's a good book there; can you read it?"

"Oh, yes. I read it every day. Look here in the cover. That's my father's and my mother's name. 'Thomas Cook married to Elizabeth Allen, 1607, Scrooby, Nottinghamshire. Born of this union, Peter, 1608.' That's me."

"Peter Cook, eh? Don't recollect the name. Wait now, weren't there some Allens and Cooks who used to go to Pastor Robinson's meetings in the church before they were forbidden?"

"I don't know about that, sir."

"His mother, old Mrs. Robinson, lives hard by the church this very day. Nine, ten years ago Pastor Robinson took all his people to Holland."

"You mean they all went there—whole families?"

"That's right. Whole families. They're probably all Dutchmen by this time."

"I think it would be fun to go to some other country. Why did they go?"

"Oh, some fuss over religion. Didn't like bowing and scraping, and all that."

The carter lowered his voice and looked around, although there was no one in sight on road or field. "They wanted to read the Bible more. Against the Established Church, it was. Pastor Robinson took to preaching in people's haymows and cellars. Townspeople set watch night and day. Quiet folk, his people, but they didn't much like being watched. Pastor Robinson took them all to Holland."

"I'm going to Holland myself someday." Peter was surprised at his own words, but he knew they were true.

The carter looked at him oddly. "Strange thing about Pastor Robinson's mother. He couldn't pry her loose from her herb garden and her cellar full of cures. She's there now; makes a pretty penny curing people."

Peter knew all of a sudden that Mrs. Robinson was the person he would visit in Scrooby.

"Lad, didn't your folks tell you about these Sep-a-ra-tists?"

"My parents are dead."

"Dead? Who's keeping you, then? And in such fine clothes"

"Master was."

"Was? Did something happen to him?"

"He died yesterday."

The carter turned, his eyes squinting with suspicion. "Why didn't the mistress take charge?"

"She didn't come back. None of them came back."

"Back from where?"

"London."

The carter scratched his leg with his whip. "Something mighty sudden must have taken master, mistress, and all, at one time."

"It was the plague." Peter blurted out the truth.

The carter's face turned white. He moved away from Peter as far as he could without falling off the seat.

"Were you around him? I mean, did you touch him or anything?"

"Oh, yes. I tried to drag him to the house, but I wasn't strong enough."

The carter jumped to the ground. "The plague? The black death? Oh, mercy, mercy on us all. Please, good

19

Peter Cook, go away. Don't come to Scrooby. In the name of God's mercy, have pity on my five children. I'll not be the bearer of death to my little ones. I'll put an armload of rosemary in the cart. They say that's good for plague. I'll go to Mrs. Robinson—she'll tell me what herbs to burn. . . ." He babbled on, gesturing for Peter to get down.

Peter was so astonished at first that he sat with open mouth, trying to make sense of the words. Only when the carter lifted his whip did Peter, still staring, toss his bundle over the side and jump down from the cart.

His voice quavered. "I'm sorry, sir."

The carter flicked his horse with the whip. The wheels squeaked as the cart rocked from side to side down the road. A cloud of dust settled on Peter as he slowly picked up his bundle.

Hours later, Peter walked through a little town with narrow cobbled streets and apartments overhanging the shops beneath. A group of schoolboys surrounded a sturdy, sandy-haired boy. He stood with folded arms and tightened lips as the other boys jeered and hooted at him. The ringleader of the group raised his hand. "The preacher will now give us a sermon."

The boy called "preacher" did not move.

"Come on, preacher. You're a Separatist. Separate a few words from yourself."

The boys laughed. Someone caught sight of Peter and beckoned the others.

"My name's Duke," the leader said. "What's yours?"

"Peter Cook."

"That's a funny way to carry your schoolbooks. Or is it your washing?" The boys laughed. "Let's see your hands."

Peter had washed in a stream near the town. He held up clean hands.

"No ink stain. Didn't you go to school today?"

"No. I'm traveling."

"Where to?"

"Scrooby."

"What for?"

"Visiting."

"Your folks live there?"

"My folks are dead."

"Who gave you all those fine clothes?"

"The master did."

"Where does he live?"

"He's dead too."

"Hunting accident?"

"No. The plague." This time Peter spoke the words deliberately.

Duke's eyes widened. He held up both arms and backed the group away. With his eyes still on Peter, he drew a line on the cobblestones and challenged him, "Don't step over this."

The word *plague* passed from boy to boy. Duke beckoned, and the boys ran down the street into the shops. Shopkeepers came out and stared at Peter. Soon shutters and shop doors closed.

Peter was alone on the street.

But not quite alone. The boy with sandy hair had watched. Now he walked toward Peter with a smile.

"You saw those cowards disappear?" He nodded scornfully. "I'm not afraid."

"I thought everyone was afraid of the plague. Why aren't you?"

"Because I believe that when God means for us to

die, we'll die. There's a time for everything. That's what the Bible says."

"Don't you belong to the Established Church?" Peter asked.

"No, indeed, I'm a Separatist."

"Why aren't you and your parents in Holland?"

The other boy stopped short. "But they are in Holland. How did you know anything about Holland?"

Peter explained.

"So your name is Peter Cook. Mine is Elbert Farham. My parents went to Holland with Pastor Robinson. I have a scholarship here. It's the school Elder Brewster went to—he's one of the elders in the church. He knows the headmaster of the school. The boys here tease me because I want to be a preacher. You notice they don't fight me, though. I licked them all one by one." He looked Peter up and down. "If you ever had to fight, I don't think you'd have much of a chance."

"My master taught me how to use a sword, not fists."

"Oh, he did? That won't help you now. By the way, where will you sleep tonight?"

"I don't know," Peter said.

"If you had kept still about the plague, I could have you as a guest at supper, but that's out. You can't go walking up the Great North Road tonight. That's out too." Elbert snapped his fingers. "I have it. I'm usher at table this week, so I can sneak you a bit of something to eat for supper. You can sleep in the cowshed out back. Come on. I'll show you before the others return."

Elbert led the way past the school building to the shed and showed Peter his hiding place in the loft. "I come here when I get tired of being teased. Stay right here until I come back."

The food Elbert brought was delicious. The boy gave final instructions to Peter. "Be on your way by daybreak. Look for the church steeple. You can't miss it. Good-by, and good luck."

As Elbert had said, the church was easy to find, but Peter was tired from hours of walking when he reached Scrooby. Near the church he heard someone chopping wood behind a little house.

"Child, you startled me," a voice called out as Peter rounded the corner. Peter saw an old woman, toothless, but with twinkling eyes. A clean white kerchief covered her hair, and she wore a white apron over her dark dress.

"I don't think I know you," she said, brushing her hands on her apron. "Come closer. Let's have a look. Ah, that mouth—the Allen mouth, always smiling—and that long slender face, the Cook face, as I'm alive! But there are no more Cooks and Allens in Scrooby. Who are you?"

"I'm Peter Cook."

At first Peter left out about the plague, but he felt impelled to tell everything, even if the old woman sent him away.

She nodded at his story. "Ay, yes. People worry about the wrong things. Plagues, pestilence, famine what difference does it make? When the Lord wants us, He'll take us. This carter you told about he came running to me yesterday. I told him to come back today. I made him a potion with vinegar, a little wormwood, and powdered eggshells. That'll make him think twice about catching the plague."

Peter laughed.

"Mrs. Robinson, why didn't you go to Holland with the others?"

"Me? I was too old to transplant in new soil." She

smiled in toothless good humor. "Peter, I have an idea. Why don't you live with me? You have no one, and I have no one. . . . Why, what's the matter?"

Peter stared past her toward the road. "Oh, Mrs. Robinson, it's the carter coming. He'll see me and turn me over to the constable. I just know he will. What shall I do?"

Mrs. Robinson pushed him in front of her. "I'll just tuck you in my herb cellar for safekeeping. My son John used to hide down there so much it's a wonder he didn't sprout roots."

She led Peter to a door made so cleverly that it looked like a beam of the house.

"Mind the steps there. Look out for the vinegar crock, and don't brush the dried herbs off the wall."

Peter's nostrils prickled at the spicy smell of the dark cellar. He sniffed cinnamon, cloves, nutmeg, dried violets, and sage. He recognized some of the herbs—dried ivyberries, rue, and his favorite, the mayflower.

The carter's voice rumbled upstairs. "I'll have the law on that boy. The constable will put him in the pesthouse where he belongs—going around carrying plague."

"Take a spoonful of this," Peter heard Mrs. Robinson say. "It's the best preventive in the world for plague."

The carter coughed and spluttered. "The plague itself couldn't be worse, Mrs. Robinson."

"A spoonful a day for three weeks. Burn these sweet herbs on the hearth every day. Doing this will drive the pestilence from the air."

"Thank 'ee Mrs. Robinson. It's a dear cure, it is. I'll drop a word in the constable's ear to be on the lookout for that boy. Good day."

24

Later, over a delicious supper, Peter almost forgot the carter's threat until a horse neighed. Mrs. Robinson shook her head in warning, motioned Peter to the corner of the kitchen, and lifted a woven mat. Peter helped her open a trap door to the herb cellar. Mrs. Robinson handed Peter a lighted candle, put her fingers to her lips. Just as she lowered the trap door, someone banged on the front door.

A deep strong voice roared, "Open, in the name of the king."

BOY LOST

Peter held his breath. The footsteps overhead sounded like an army. He heard the voices of two different men. One had a low, rich voice, and the other spoke fast and clearly. Peter strained to catch the words. There was a burst of laughter, and Mrs. Robinson talked in such excitement that her words ran together. Peter could not understand anything.

Now she's telling the constable and the watchman about me, he thought. In a minute they'll open the trap door.

Where could he go this time? It was night. He thought of taking one of the horses, but that would be stealing. Surely it wasn't wrong to help a man dying of plague. Peter could not see how he had done anything wrong at all.

He snuffed out the candle, picked up his bundle, and pushed the cellar door open. He crouched ready to plunge outside at the first sound.

"Let's have a look at the little fellow." The man with the low, throaty voice boomed out the words with a chuckle.

Peter heard the trap door open. He bounded outside and looked wildly around for a hiding place. The moonlight grew brighter every minute. The outlines of the church loomed up on the other side of the house. The church yes, that was it. He gasped in relief. There would be many places to hide in Scrooby church. But as he started to run, his feet sank into the moist garden plot where Mrs. Robinson's young vegetables and herbs were growing. He must not ruin them.

His feet sank deeper into the mud. Just as the cellar door opened, he jerked free and dived for the overgrown hedgerow. He twisted and squirmed into a hollow space in the prickly hedge. The blood throbbed in his ears and throat, and he gulped air in frantic gasps.

He heard Mrs. Robinson call to the men, "Don't walk across my new garden."

"He can't be too far away. There's no place to go. But I don't see him." The man with the clear voice sounded alarmed.

Peter lay on his stomach with his eyes shut. His muscles cramped from strain, but he did not dare move. Although it was a warm night, he shivered.

"Maybe he's in the church."

"That's it! We should have thought of it sooner! He's probably at the top of the steeple by this time."

"Now, boys, not through my garden. Come back through the house," Mrs. Robinson said.

27

The voices grew fainter. Peter relaxed and curled up with his bundle under his head. After a long time the horses neighed as they were ridden off into the night. Still Peter did not stir. Some distance away, a man began to shout a phrase over and over. It was the town crier.

Peter crept out and ran from bush to fence, grass tuft to tree, looking over his shoulder. The town crier's lantern swung from side to side as he chanted the news to each cottage.

"Boy lost—boy lost. Peter Cook, age ten."

Windows were unlatched. Nightcapped heads peered out. There were exclamations. Some voices were gruff, some sympathetic. A woman cried out in pity, "Oh, the poor lonely little boy." At one cottage the owner questioned the crier.

"Who is it?"

"Peter Cook, age ten."

"Hasn't been a Cook family in Scrooby these nine, ten years. All dead." The man latched the window.

At the edge of town the crier turned back. Peter waited until the lantern light was only a glimmer before he headed for the Great North Road. It unwound like an endless ribbon in the full moonlight. Miles and hours later, Peter reached the shelter of the loft where Elbert Farham had told him he could sleep. He flung himself on the straw and slept until the neighing of horses woke him.

Two men were talking underneath him. Terror and despair swept over Peter. He recognized the voices of the night before.

"If we go on to the inn this evening we won't have to pay for the horses another night." The man with the low voice made everything sound like a joke.

The other man sounded troubled. "I wish we could find the boy."

"When he gets hungry enough, he will go back."

Peter was shaking so much he thought the men would hear the rustling of the straw. It was no use to keep running away, he decided. Besides, he had no place to go.

"I'm ready," he called as he climbed down. He saw a stocky man dressed in brown, with a broad, pleasant face. The other man was dark-haired and slim, with a slight stoop. He wore a blue coat and a violet-and-green waistcoat.

Peter brushed the straw off his clothes and straightened his collar. He looked up at the men.

"I'm ready now."

The stocky man spoke in a gentle voice. "The boy we're looking for doesn't go to school here."

"I don't go to school here."

"But your face looks familiar, somehow. Do I know your parents?"

"You did, sir. I'm Peter Cook."

In their surprise both men repeated his name. The stocky man put a hand on Peter's shoulder. "I'm Pastor Robinson, and this is Elder Brewster."

"You're Pastor Robinson?" Peter's voice was so unbelieving that both men smiled. "Are you going to arrest me?"

"Why no, Peter. What on earth for?"

"Last night I heard you say, 'Open in the name of the king.'"

Pastor Robinson shouted with laughter, then caught himself and spoke sympathetically. "So that's why you ran away! That explains the mystery. You see, my mother and I have this joke. When I lived in Scrooby, I used to have to hide in the cellar to keep from being arrested. When I visit my mother now, I always bang on the door and say, 'Open in the name of the king.' It gives her a delicious fright, and then we have a good laugh."

Peter discovered he could swallow again.

"But, Peter, where did you go? We looked all over the church." Elder Brewster spoke with comic dismay.

"I started there, but I didn't dare walk across Mrs. Robinson's new garden."

The men laughed so hard Peter was annoyed, and then he joined in.

"And then what, Peter?"

"I waited awhile and came here." Peter told how he had met Elbert Farham.

"Well, Peter, I'm very glad you're found. Mother wants you to live with her, and I think it would be a fine thing. You could help her with the garden—keeping weeds and people out of it." Pastor Robinson winked. Peter could tell he loved to joke. "Would you like that?"

Peter gulped. He wanted to say, "I'd rather go with you," but it did not sound polite. At this moment Elbert burst in to greet Pastor Robinson and Elder Brewster. His mouth dropped open at the sight of Peter.

Peter envied Elbert. He was already a Separatist, and he could go to Holland any time he wanted.

The two boys followed the men to the headmaster's library. [The headmaster was the school principal.] The man's slender beard waggled with excitement as he talked.

"What you ought to do is get out of Holland, Pastor Robinson. Go someplace where you can do as you please. Now, the New World is just the place." He picked up a book. "Have you seen Captain Smith's *Description of New England?* I know the man personally. Why don't you ask him about it?"

Pastor Robinson drummed his fingers on the table. "We've been thinking along these lines for some time. Holland has been kind, but our children work too hard for too little. That is the price we are paying for religious freedom."

The headmaster leaned back in his chair. "You'll become a Dutch citizen one of these days. You talk like a Dutchman now."

Pastor Robinson flushed but said nothing.

Elbert took Peter to one side. "Don't say a word about the plague at dinner tonight. The others won't dare say anything to the headmaster. But be on your guard. These boys love revenge."

At dinnertime Peter was placed next to Duke, the ringleader of the day before. Duke scowled and knocked Peter's elbow so that his little loaf of bread skidded to the floor. Elbert, with flashing eyes, brought another loaf. "Be careful and look out," he warned.

When Elbert brought in water for the hand washing, he stumbled over Duke's outstretched foot and upset the water. Elbert turned scarlet, glanced at Duke, and went without a word to get a cloth. Peter heard smothered giggles around the table.

At the end of the meal, Duke spoke to the headmaster. "Please, sir, may we ask our guest to honor us with grace?"

"Why, yes. Peter, will you say grace?"

Peter felt every eye on him, but did not hesitate or stumble over the Latin phrases. When he finished, there was absolute silence in the room.

31

After dinner Pastor Robinson called to him. "Peter, the headmaster is much impressed with your Latin, so much so that he is offering you a scholarship. Would you like to go to school here?"

"Oh, sir, I—I don't know what to say."

"I can quite understand that. Everything has been going pretty fast for you. Why don't you talk it over with Elbert? He's a level-headed boy. Don't you find him so?" Pastor Robinson turned back to the headmaster.

Peter found Elbert outside, standing by himself.

"Elbert, shall I go to school here?"

Elbert beamed. "That would be fine, Peter." He nudged Peter in warning. Duke was approaching them.

"You think you're smart with all that Latin, don't you?" Duke stood with feet apart and raised his fists. The boys gathered around and cleared a circle for the two.

Peter eyed his taller rival. He saw at once that quickness was his only defense. Using his hand and arm like a sword, he parried and thrust as he had been taught, avoiding Duke's slow, powerful blows by eel-like twists. He dodged and darted, his eyes never leaving Duke's face. The taller boy stood like a stone wall until he made the mistake Peter looked for—reaching with both hands. In that split second when Duke reached down, Peter opened his hand and swung up on the other boy's chin. Caught off guard, Duke crashed to the ground and lay rubbing his jaw. Peter held out his hand and helped Duke to his feet.

"Bully good show," someone said, and the others applauded.

"Are you going to school here now?"

The boys crowded around in friendly fashion.

"I'm not sure yet." Peter felt that the boys liked him

now. He felt good inside. But he still wanted to go to Holland.

Pastor Robinson, Elder Brewster, and the headmaster came outside, talking with such seriousness Peter did not want to interrupt.

"I don't know what it is about you Separatists," the headmaster said. "I won't argue about your religious beliefs, but mark my words, Elder Brewster is going to get into a lot of trouble one of these days with his printing press. Oh, I know why you come over on 'business' trips to distribute the books you have printed against the church. But what I started to say was about Peter. I think he can have quite a career here in England. We'll send him to Cambridge University, of course."

Pastor Robinson protested. "You sound as if there weren't any other university in the world. Leyden University in Holland isn't exactly unknown, you know. Elder Brewster and I are students there now. He teaches, too. Incidentally, do you remember William Bradford? Since he's been in Holland he has mastered five languages—Dutch, French, Latin, Greek, and Hebrew."

"Why Hebrew?"

"He was afraid he might be missing something if he didn't read the Old Testament in the original tongue."

The headmaster clucked. "That's what I mean about you Separatists—you and your peculiar ideas. I suggest that Brewster learn Hebrew and print his tracts and books in that language. It would be safer."

Peter cleared his throat, and the men looked at him. "Pastor Robinson?"

"Yes, Peter. Have you decided? Are you going to my mother's or are you going to stay here and go to school?"

"Please, sir. Neither."

"Neither?" There was silence.

"Please, sir, I want to go to Holland with you."

There was another silence.

"But Peter, we went to Holland because we had a strong belief about the worship of God."

"I know."

"Our children must work like men and women just to live. You are not very big."

"But I know what work is. I'm not afraid of it. I want to be there with you and the others. If my parents had lived. . . ." Peter's eyes filled with tears.

"Yes, Peter." Pastor Robinson's voice was gentle. "If your parents had lived, you would be there now."

He was quiet so long that Peter gave up hope.

"Very well, Peter, go get your things. We're leaving immediately."

Peter ran to tell Elbert the news. Duke kept a safe distance away.

"So now we have two Separatists. You're going to separate together. Is that it?" the boys sneered. The friendliness that they had shown after the fight was all gone. Peter stood baffled and insecure. In a panic, he turned to Elbert.

"Is this what it means to be a Separatist? Everybody is against you?"

Elbert smiled. "You'll get used to it. But you've got to believe in something mighty hard not to let it bother you. It's not too late. You could go back to Scrooby."

"No, I want to go to Holland."

In a little while Peter mounted a horse behind Elder Brewster and said good-by to Elbert. As they rode off, Peter heard a soft hissing from the boys. It sounded like "S-S-S," with a final, scornful "Separatist."

The next twelve hours passed like a dream—the jolting ride to the inn, the fat landlord whose big grin of welcome faded when he saw the poverty of his guests, the tiny rush-covered room where they slept, hardly better than the hayloft at the school. But when Peter saw the sails of the ship they were to board, he skipped down the sloping steps of the dock two at a time.

"Peter, if you don't keep your feet on the ground you'll be flying to Holland."

The Dutch captain stood on deck. He checked Pastor Robinson's and Elder Brewster's Dutch permits.

"And where is the boy's permit?"

"He doesn't have one, but he's with us."

"Your son?"

"No."

"This other man's son?"

"No."

"Any relation?"

"No."

The captain's cheeks puffed in anger and his skin showed red and white. "You want to get me in trouble with the English?" He paced the deck. "You want me to lose my ship? Rot in jail somewhere? I've got a big family to support."

The captain pounded the rail to emphasize each word. "No permit, no passage."

"But what can we do?"

The captain shrugged and showed the palms of his hands. "Send the boy back where he came from."

Chapter Four

SMUGGLED TO FREEDOM

The Dutch captain folded his arms across his broad chest.

"Gentlemen, the tide is rising. We're almost ready to sail."

Without a word Pastor Robinson and Elder Brewster turned away.

"Aren't you going to sail, Pastor Robinson?"

"Yes, but we have a little thinking to do." At the dockside Pastor Robinson set his hand luggage down with a thump.

"I don't want to cause any trouble," Peter said. "I'm sure I could find my way back to the school all right."

"What? You want to separate from the Separatists already?" Peter knew from Pastor Robinson's smile that he had overheard the boys at school. "Peter, you're our little lost sheep. We won't abandon you."

Pastor Robinson sat down on his luggage and rested his chin in his hand. Suddenly he slapped his knee and laughed. "William," he said, looking up at Elder Brewster, "I remember a traveling cape that you once had. It covered you from head to foot, and everyone used to laugh about it." Elder Brewster reached for a neatly wrapped bundle. "I always take it in case of rain. Why?"

"Let's have a look at it. I think we're going to have a little more hand luggage than usual this trip."

Elder Brewster stared for a minute, then began to laugh. Peter was puzzled.

"Suppose we just step behind these." Pastor Robinson pointed to a pile of barrels on the dock. Elder Brewster opened his pack and pulled out his gabardine traveling cape. Pastor Robinson spread it out flat, looked around, and beckoned to Peter.

"Now, Peter, just lie down in the middle of this cape. Draw your knees up and clasp them with your hands."

Peter did so.

"Do you think you can stay like that for a few minutes and not cry out if you are bumped once in a while?"

"Oh, yes."

"Now, William, you pay all three fares. I'm sure the captain will allow us this extra luggage."

He wrapped Peter in the cape, leaving a hole for air and making a loose handle of the folds.

Peter felt himself being lifted. He tried not to squirm as he was swung down the steps of the dock. He bumped first against Pastor Robinson's sturdy legs and then against Elder Brewster's thin ones. The men grunted a little with the strain.

"You have quite a load there." The captain's voice

was very smooth. "Don't you want my men to toss it in the hold?"

"Oh, no, thank you. We—uh—have some personal things we may need on the trip. Sorry about the boy, Captain. Hope it didn't cause you any inconvenience."

"You are very generous, gentlemen." Peter sensed that the captain had counted the three fares and was bowing. He felt himself being swung down steps. Pastor Robinson untied the cape and grinned at Peter, who un-kinked his legs and looked around the tiny cubicle of a cabin. Peter did not see the water once on the whole trip. In Holland he left the ship in the same way.

Pastor Robinson kept chuckling about the luggage. "I thought once you were going to trip all of us right into the sea," he told Elder Brewster as they started toward Leyden.

But Peter was too excited about his first sight of Holland to do more than smile at the pastor's jokes. The flat-faced houses and level land were so different from the bulging cottages and rolling countryside of England.

Pastor Robinson explained that the Separatists lived in Choir Alley, a street of twenty-one houses that they owned. No one was in sight when they arrived.

"Isn't anybody home?" Peter asked.

"Just women with babies. Everyone has to work, Peter."

"But where's the church?"

Pastor Robinson pointed to a house longer than the rest.

"It's in my house. We live on the top floor, and the meeting room is underneath. It's seventy-five feet long."

The houses were joined together side to side. When the travelers came to Elder Brewster's house, the upper half of the door opened a crack. A tall, slender woman peeked out, gasped, and opened the whole door.

"Oh, I was hoping you would stay in England for a while. It's starting all over again—the prying, the spying, the informers. Oh, William, they searched the houses one by one. If your printing press hadn't been so heavy, I would have buried it myself in the backyard. Now it's gone. They took it away."

Elder Brewster turned pale as he stared at his wife. She flung her arms around his neck and burst into tears. "But that's not the worst of it. There's a warrant for your arrest because of the last book. I heard that the English ambassador swears he will have you jailed."

The words were hardly spoken when a heavy rap sounded on the door. A group of Dutch officials murmured apologies, and a search officer unrolled a paper. "William Brewster, you are charged with printing and circulating in England fifteen religious tracts against the church. Your embassy has requested us to place you under arrest immediately."

Elder Brewster kissed his wife and left.

Pastor Robinson waited until the group was out of sight. "Mrs. Brewster, will you look after Peter? I have to go to the university."

"Of course, Pastor Robinson."

In spite of the warm day, Peter shivered. Mrs. Brewster hustled him to the kitchen. She cooked a hot meal for him and listened to his story.

"You have made a brave choice, Peter. It's true, as you can see, that we still have troubles, but they are as nothing compared to what we have gained. To worship God as we choose is worth more than life itself. God asks a great deal of us, but He gives us the strength to

accomplish His purposes." The heat of the fire and her excitement made her cheeks glow.

Someone knocked at the door.

"What more do they want?" Mrs. Brewster sighed.

To Peter's surprise, Pastor Robinson and Elder Brewster walked in.

"William! Pastor Robinson! What happened?"

"Students of Leyden University cannot be arrested. It's the law. I just happened to remember about it." Pastor Robinson beamed with satisfaction.

Elder Brewster did not look so cheerful as the pastor. He stared glumly at the kitchen fire.

"There's just one thing," he said. "No one seems to

41

know what became of my printing press. Everywhere I asked, all the answer I got was, 'What printing press'?"

Pastor Robinson frowned. "I heard that the English ambassador won't stop until you're in jail. It may be necessary for you to go into hiding at Scrooby. The cellar is a pretty good hiding place, don't you think so, Peter?"

Peter felt himself blush.

"Pastor," Elder Brewster said, ignoring the pastor's joke, "you told us any number of times that if a sign were given, we would leave Holland and live somewhere else."

"Yes, I remember." Pastor Robinson began to pace with his hands behind his back. "This looks like the writing on the wall. Let's settle the question once and for all tonight. We'll have to tell everyone. Would you like to come with us, Peter?"

They found some of the Separatists washing fleeces in the canal. Others were carding wool with brushes. Still others were reeling yarn on large wheels. About twenty weavers were making coarse, thick cloth. Besides these, Peter met a tailor, a hatter, a cobbler, and a brickmason. Children helped their parents.

William Bradford, the man who knew five languages, was dyeing silk. Peter was struck by his paleness. He was so puny he looked as though he would collapse if someone put a hand on him. Pastor Robinson gave him a hearty slap on the shoulder, and William Bradford bent nearly double.

By the time everyone had been notified of the meeting, it was almost dark.

"How long does everybody work?" Peter asked when he saw that no one was preparing to quit.

"From twelve to fifteen hours a day. Children too."

Pastor Robinson shook his head. "It isn't good. We know that. I hope and pray that we can make the right decision tonight."

About a hundred people came to Pastor Robinson's house after dark. The men sat on one side and the women on the other. After Pastor Robinson explained about Elder Brewster's arrest, he opened the meeting for discussion.

"We all know that Holland is preparing for war. 'A wise man seeth the plague when it cometh and hideth himself.' Now the question is, What shall we do?"

A tailor spoke. "Our children grow old before their time from hard work. Why don't we become Dutch citizens so that we can join the guilds and have better jobs?"

A weaver stood up. "Pastor Robinson, you signed your name *Jan Roberts* in the register. That's the Dutch way. Do you plan to become a Dutch citizen?"

Pastor Robinson shook his head. "I have always tried to conform with the Dutch ways as much as possible. Holland has been very kind to us."

A wool comber arose. "Let's go to some other land."

A silk maker objected. "We would have to sell everything we own to raise the money."

Another weaver suggested, "Let's make a colony in Guiana. It's warm there. They say it is always springtime."

"There are always diseases too," the cobbler said. "A hot country always has diseases."

Questions and answers came fast. Peter stretched and twisted, trying to see the speakers.

"Why don't we go to Virginia? The English are already there."

"What? And be under the British thumb? We might as well go back to England."

"Let's go to Florida."

"Yes, and be killed by the Spaniards, like the French!"

"Let's go to some place in America that has not been settled yet."

This suggestion pleased the majority. Before the meeting ended, it was decided to send messengers to England to obtain the king's seal of approval for the religious freedom of the Separatists in the New World.

Pastor Robinson held up his hand for silence. "Great actions are accompanied by great difficulties, and overcome with great courage. Our mission is to advance the kingdom of Christ. We can expect the blessing of God on our undertaking."

As the meeting ended, there was a buzz of talk. People discussed selling their houses, raising money, and gathering supplies for the move to the new country. Peter was excited.

The two messengers, John Carver and Robert Cushman, spent weeks in England. When they returned, the news they brought was passed from door to door, from canal to weaver's loom.

"The king won't grant us religious freedom."

"Pastor Robinson," Peter asked, "does that mean we can't go to America?"

The pastor looked tired and discouraged. "We can't give up our religious freedom, and if the king won't let us have it in America, we'll have to stay in Holland."

STRANDED

Once again Pastor Robinson's meeting room buzzed with voices, this time subdued. Peter looked around at the gloomy faces. Only Pastor Robinson had recovered his usual cheerfulness, and he spoke firmly.

"I know we are all disappointed because the king will not grant his seal. Even if we had a seal as broad as the floor, the king could reverse his decision even if he had granted approval and then regretted it. My friends, remember this: We are not beset with difficulties in order to yield to them, but to overcome them with God's help." The pastor's rich, confident voice rang through the room.

"Pastor Robinson, do you remember our Amsterdam friends who sailed to Virginia?" It was Robert Cushman, one of the London messengers speaking this time.

"Yes, and I predicted no good would come of the attempt. Their leader denied God's Holy Word."

"Well, Pastor, they were packed like herrings in the ship and didn't have enough water or the proper food. Out of a hundred and eighty people, a hundred and thirty died."

Pastor Robinson bowed his head for a moment. When he spoke again his voice was calm, but Peter saw that his face had paled. "That means that we must have a large enough ship and sufficient food and supplies to last a year at least."

"Pastor," a button maker called out, "how are we going to make a living in a savage country like America?"

The pastor's answer was unhesitating. "By fishing. It is an honest trade. It was the apostles' own calling."

There was a disturbance in the back of the room. Every head turned. A group of Dutchmen had come in and stood waiting.

"I'm sorry," the pastor said. "This is a private meeting." He went to show the men out.

But after a conversation which Peter could not hear, Pastor Robinson led the men to the front of the room.

"These gentlemen have an offer to make. I have told them that all our decisions are voted on. The men are willing to take the chance." The pastor twinkled as he nodded to them.

A portly man stepped out of the group. "We are businessmen here in Leyden. It has come to our ears that you are planning to colonize in America. We offer you a ship, food, and supplies, including cattle, if you will colonize in our name on the Hudson River."

"But we would be the same as Dutch citizens. We

want our children to be English," someone said. After some discussion the congregation voted down the offer. The Dutch businessmen left, shaking their heads and talking to one another.

The next morning Mrs. Brewster thrust a manuscript into Peter's hands. "Run to the university with this, will you, Peter? My husband is supposed to give a lecture this morning. These are his notes."

Peter found Elder Brewster in the university library, a large room with eleven double rows of bookshelves. Elder Brewster was sitting on a stool reading, and the book was chained to the reading ledge.

As Peter placed the manuscript in front of him, Elder Brewster clapped his hand to his forehead. "Oh, thank you, Peter. Mrs. Brewster tells me I will forget my head someday."

On the way home Peter watched a man hobbling along the street, and he couldn't help staring at him. Everything he had on was the biggest of its kind Peter had ever seen, from the beaver hat with a large silver buckle, a yellow doublet with slashed sleeves, the lace cuffs and collar so wide they almost met, to the round jeweled buttons (at least twelve) that glittered on the front of his jacket. A huge ring decorated the forefinger of his left hand. The man wore his brown hair in fat ringlets on either side of his curly beard. His nose looked pinched, and his eyes were quick and darting.

"You, boy, what's your name?" the man asked, pointing with his ring finger.

"Peter Cook."

"You live in this neighborhood?" He pointed again, this time at the houses.

"Yes, sir."

"One of the Separatists, by any chance?"

"Yes, sir."

"Good. You can help me. I just arrived from England. I'm looking for a Pastor Robinson. My foot is killing me. It has been swelling ever since I got off the ship. Here, just let me put my hand on your shoulder, that's a good boy. Now, lead on, not too fast."

Peter found Pastor Robinson at home, and the man introduced himself. "I'm Thomas Weston. I have an offer which may interest you." He looked over the large, plain meeting room into which Peter had led him. "Here, boy, help me get my foot up on the bench. Don't go away, I'll need you later; you're just the right size. I hope all the Separatists are as useful."

Pastor Robinson smiled. "Peter has made himself useful in many ways, but this is the first time he's been a crutch."

"Now, Pastor Robinson, the word has got around about your people wanting to colonize. My business friends and I—we call ourselves the Adventurers—are willing to back such an enterprise. What you do is this: Sign a contract for seven years. Establish a permanent trading post in America. Trade for furs and fish. Work for us four days of the week and two days for yourselves. We Adventurers will outfit you completely. How does this sound?"

Mr. Weston opened a leather pouch, took out a hollow bowl with a long stem, and stuffed it with dark brown leaves. Pastor Robinson and Peter exchanged startled looks.

"Do you mind if I smoke?" Mr. Weston sucked on the hollow stem and puffed smoke rings from his mouth. "Well, what do you say about my proposition?"

48

"It sounds fine, Mr. Weston, but my congregation will have to vote on it. I can call a general meeting for tonight, if you would care to present your idea then."

"Can't wait—can't wait. Tell you what I'll do. I'll contact a few of your head men and let them work on the others. You can let me know your decision by messenger, and we can work out more details of the contract."

Pastor Robinson agreed. "Peter, since you know where everyone is working, perhaps you would be Mr. Weston's crutch for as long as he needs you."

Mr. Weston leaned on Peter as they left the house.

Mr. Weston warned every Separatist, "Now, don't meddle with the Dutch, and don't sign up with the Virginia Company. Let me handle these things."

At the canal Mr. Weston sat down on a pile of dry fleeces to rest. Puffs of smoke came from his mouth as he drew on his pipe.

There was a stir of consternation among the workers washing the fleeces.

"The man's on fire!"

"It's the devil himself at work."

"One spark, and those fleeces will be ruined."

"It's a new custom called smoking," Peter said, but he was too late. Two men had taken Mr. Weston by the arms and two by the legs. Before he could remove his pipe from his mouth, the men had swung him into the canal. He came up choking and flailing his arms. His pipe was still clamped between his teeth. All his finery clung to him. His brown hair lay matted against his head, and his beard hung in strings.

"You fools! Ignoramuses! Don't you know anything about fashion?" Mr. Weston sputtered. He tried to peel off his jacket, but the wet material clung to his arms and

he stood with his hands caught behind his back, unable to move. He sneezed his pipe into the canal. Peter fished it out and then helped pull the wet jacket off Mr. Weston who then sat down to dry in the sun.

"At least my foot feels better," he said, touching it gently. He noticed that everyone had gathered around him. "Now about my offer . . . ." When he had explained it, the Separatists thought it was a good one.

"We must decide who is to go on the first trip and

who is to go later," Pastor Robinson said at the next meeting, when the vote carried. "I'll go with the majority—or stay, as the case may be. In order for us to know God's will, in proper humility, let us fast tomorrow."

The next day Pastor Robinson took as his text Ezra 8:21: "Then I proclaimed a fast there, at the river of Ahava, that we might afflict ourselves before our God, to seek of him a right way for us, and for our little ones, and for all our substance."

When the meeting was opened for discussion, opinions came from all sides.

"I want to go, but I can't sell my house right away."

"There isn't a ship big enough to take us all."

"How shall we govern ourselves over there as a church?"

Pastor Robinson was decisive about this. "Each group will have to be independent, each an absolute church unto itself. It might well be that we shall never see one another again."

After the day of fasting and prayer, a vote was taken. By a slight majority, most voted to go on the second trip, not the first. Peter felt sorry for Pastor Robinson, and the pastor could not hide his disappointment.

Working out the plans to go to America took months. Peter lost track of the trips the messengers took back and forth to England. Then Robert Cushman returned with bad news.

"Mr. Weston says the Adventurers insist on six days' labor instead of four."

Peter saw Pastor Robinson angry for once. "But that will make the Separatists slaves. You didn't agree, I hope?"

Robert Cushman hesitated. "What could I do? If I said 'No,' they would have taken back their money."

"Did you sign anything?"

"Well, yes, I did."

At the next meeting there was much criticism of Mr. Cushman's action.

"You had no right to sign such an agreement. I'm going to withdraw right now," some said.

"Let's leave without signing anything," others said.

"Just what is in this contract?" William Bradford demanded.

The messenger explained. "The main change is that everything the planters build or improve will be used in common. All profits will be in common stock. At the end of seven years, everything will be divided between the Adventurers and the planters, but during that time, all our laboring time will be contracted to the Adventurers."

The usually quiet Separatists rose in an uproar.

"We cannot sign this."

A few days later good news came. One of the Adventurers was willing to let the Separatists use his hundred-and-eighty-ton ship, the *Mayflower*, as part of the contract provision. Capt. Christopher Jones and an experienced mate had already been hired.

At this news all objections seemed to be forgotten. Houses were sold, money raised, and wooden chests were packed with household necessities. The Separatists bought a sixty-ton ship called the *Speedwell*. It was to remain in America to carry fish and furs along the coast.

When Elder Brewster announced to his family, "Tomorrow we start on our journey," Peter thought his heart would burst with joy. He helped pack the two hundred books Elder Brewster was taking.

Almost everyone in the congregation took the twenty-four-hour trip by canal boat to Delfshaven to say farewell to the ones who were sailing. The night of their arrival no one slept. Everyone talked all night long. When it was time for those who were leaving to board the *Speedwell*, Peter, for the first time, realized what parting meant.

Pastor Robinson fell to his knees and, with tears running down his cheeks, blessed the travelers. All knelt with him.

"Beloved brethren, we are now quickly to part from one another, and whether I may ever live to see your face on earth any more, the God of heaven only knows. You now know you are pilgrims."

On board the *Speedwell*, Peter watched the shore line with the others until he could no longer distinguish the people waving good-by. Then he turned to explore the ship, and watched the crew at work with the many ropes and sails. When the *Speedwell* arrived in Southampton four days later Peter felt the excitement of the trip. The *Mayflower* was already in the harbor, a ship three times as large as the *Speedwell*. He could not keep his eyes off it.

At the dock, the first person to meet the group was Mr. Weston, waving the articles of contract.

"Who's the leader here?"

"I am." Elder Brewster stepped forward.

"This contract must be signed."

"No, we cannot sign such terms. This is not the agreement made when you first came to us in Leyden, Mr. Weston."

"I know it—I know it." Mr. Weston was red in the face. "I'm not stupid. But the others insisted, and they are putting up the money. We must have your signature before you go. I leave it to your conscience."

"We refuse."

"All right, then. Stand on your own legs." Mr. Weston stamped off, muttering. Peter noticed he did not limp at all.

Several port officials came up. "We have here the bill for port dues."

"Port dues?" Elder Brewster sounded amazed. "How much?" He scanned the bill. "One hundred pounds? We don't have that much money left." He put his hand to his forehead. "Mr. Weston was supposed to take care of all expenses like this. Where did he go? We have all these people ready to sail. Peter, run and find Mr. Weston."

But Mr. Weston had disappeared. Peter came back and sat down on a wooden chest. He and the others looked at the *Speedwell* and *Mayflower* bobbing in the harbor. No one could board either ship until the port dues were paid, and there was no money.

STOPPED AGAIN

Elder Brewster spoke in urgent tones. "We must raise the port fees at once some way. Otherwise we won't be able to sail at all. We have neither the king's seal nor a signed contract."

John Carver stepped forward. A slow-speaking man, he chose each word with care. "As you all know, I have spent seven thousand pounds right here in Southampton for supplies. I suggest we sell some of the butter, as much as sixty or eighty firkins. We can hold an auction right here."

The Separatists agreed. Elder Brewster sent Peter and three others to announce the auction to the town's shopkeepers. On the way back Peter stopped to look at a husky young man sitting in the stocks. The young man did not seem a bit ashamed. He whistled a merry tune.

"Haven't you ever seen anyone sitting in the stocks before?" he asked as Peter stared.

"No, sir."

The young man flipped his hands. "It doesn't hurt anything except my feelings."

"What did you do wrong?"

The young man's eyes snapped. "I didn't do wrong. I was defending the Separatists."

"Oh, are you one of us?"

"I'm not a Separatist at all," the young man sighed. "They hired me as their cooper [a man who makes barrels] on a voyage that's due to start any minute. Someone made fun of my going with a bunch of crackpots, and I got into a fight over it. Now I suppose I won't get to go. Not that I really care too much, for I can get a job any place."

"They're not sailing for a while." Peter explained about the unpaid port fees. "Maybe you'll get to go after all."

"Fine. If you hear anyone ask where John Alden is, tell him I'm in the stocks. Oh, here comes that girl again."

A dark-haired girl ran up with a pewter cup full of water. Peter had seen her with the Adventurers.

"Ask the young man if he's thirsty." The girl spoke to Peter as though she had known him a long time. "I thought he might like some water." She held out the cup to Peter.

"Why don't you ask him yourself, miss?" Peter said, astonished. "He can talk. He's been talking with me."

The young man's reaction puzzled Peter. John's face had lighted up as though the gates of heaven had opened to receive him.

"Priscilla!" a sharp voice called. "Come here at once. We have to help sell butter."

"Yes, Mother."

John's eyes widened. "Are you one of them?"

The girl thrust the cup into Peter's hand. "I've got to go. Please give this to him."

"What's the matter with her?" Peter held the cup to John's lips. The young man choked on a swallow of water and did not answer.

"Do you think they'll sail before sundown?" he asked when he had finished drinking.

"I don't think so."

"Good. I'll be out of here then. You'd better go and help with that butter, don't you think?"

When Peter returned to the dock, the bidding was already under way. Six or eight strange men wearing swords surrounded Elder Brewster. They looked like military men. The leader was a strong-looking man with a sunburned face and full beard. His eyes seemed to stab in every direction. Peter edged near, fascinated.

The bearded soldier was restless. He slapped leather gloves against his thighs, touched his sword, or made sweeping movements of his hand as he talked.

"I made an offer to one of your men last year," he said.

'We appreciate your interest, Captain Smith," Elder Brewster said. "We have all read your *Description of New England* a number of times."

Captain Smith bowed. "In all modesty, I can say that I know everything that is known about the Atlantic coast. My men and I will be glad to protect you for one tenth of your first year's profits."

"I'm afraid there won't be any profits for many years," Elder Brewster said. "Everything we make has to be turned back to the company that is paying for the boat. We do have a military man with us, however. Capt. Miles Standish has joined our group on an equal basis. Perhaps you would like to do the same?"

"No, decidedly not. Too much of a gamble." Captain Smith gazed at the *Mayflower*. "It's unfortunate that you have such a leaky, unwholesome vessel."

"But it's the largest on the sea," Elder Brewster said.

"At least it's a sweet ship," the captain said and his friends laughed.

"I don't understand you, Captain Smith."

"It's a wine ship. It hauls 108 double hogsheads of wine a trip. Wine leaks, and that means a sweet ship."

Captain Smith lowered his voice and looked around. "You're sure of Captain Jones?"

"Of course. He's an experienced seaman."

Captain Smith's lips curled. "One or two fishing trips, if you call that experience." He motioned to his men and left with a curt nod of farewell.

An excited voice spoke in Peter's ear. "Wasn't that Captain Smith himself?"

Peter turned and looked into the face of Elbert Farham.

"Why, Elbert! How did you get here?" Peter was overjoyed to see his friend.

"Didn't you know I was coming? I'm going to America too. My parents sent for me. But that was Captain Smith, wasn't it? Did you know the headmaster knows him personally? Maybe he sent him here. Is he going with us?"

Peter shook his head. "We have Captain Standish."

"Which one is he?"

Peter pointed out a short man with red hair. Captain Standish was carrying the last firkin of butter to one of the townspeople. He collected the money, and with a big grin, waved it. A great cheer rose from the crowd.

"They've raised the money. Now we can sail." Peter pranced in excitement. "I hope we're on the *Mayflower*, don't you?"

Just then Elder Brewster called out, "All those from Leyden will board the *Speedwell*."

Peter felt as though the wind had been knocked out of him. He gazed with misty eyes at the *Mayflower*. He liked everything about the big ship. Made of light brown wood, with stripes of blue, yellow, and red, the *Mayflower* rode high out of the water. Her three masts supported a network of cordage and rigging. She was three times the size of the *Speedwell*.

Peter gulped down his disappointment. At least he and Elbert would be together on the trip.

"Don't look so sad, Peter. The important thing is to get there," Elbert comforted him.

Peter nodded, too miserable to say anything.

Elbert nudged him. "Look over there."

A large barrel that was being rolled across the dock had picked up so much speed that it was about to break away from its guides and plunge into the water. Elder Brewster and William Bradford rushed to block it, and a few more helping hands brought it to a standstill.

"What's in it?" someone asked. As if in answer there was a tapping sound from inside the barrel.

For the moment Peter forgot about the *Mayflower* in his amazement. He was sure there was something alive in the barrel. He held his breath as Elder Brewster and William Bradford tugged at the end of it. It broke loose with a resounding snap, and a man crawled out on all fours.

"*Merci. Merci beaucoup.* T'ank you." The man stood up, swaying, and bowed from the waist.

"Who are you?" William Bradford queried, astounded.

The man put his fingers to his lips. "It is enough to say that I come from France. I wish to sail with the Separatists. I am a Huguenot."

The crowd gasped. Peter whispered to Elbert,

"What's a Huguenot?"

"They are like us, only French."

The Frenchman rolled his eyes and pointed to where a French ship had docked a few hours before. "I arrive over there. *Voila!* I am here. I go with you?" He dropped to his knees.

"Yes! Yes !" the crowd exclaimed.

A hulking seaman from the *Mayflower* watched the scene. He stood with legs far apart, hands on hips.

"A weaker lot I've never seen," he growled as the boys came near. "If I don't help cast half of them overboard, dead, within three weeks, my name is not Ralph Bean. You, boy, how'd you like to be a shark's dinner?"

"What's a shark?" Peter asked.

"What's a shark, indeed?" Ralph Bean put his thumbs through the armholes of his sleeveless jacket and rocked back on his heels. "A shark, my boy, is a fish half as long as that little ship over there, with teeth as long as a sword. God is my witness to that."

He jerked off his knit cap and flourished it.

"One roll of the ship too far sideways and you're skidding right into Mr. Shark's jaws. Even God couldn't pry you loose." He opened his mouth wide and snapped it shut. Peter winced and shivered. In imagination he was already in the shark's mouth.

Elbert tugged at Peter's arm. "Don't listen, Peter. This man blasphemes God."

A seaman from the *Speedwell* paused in his loading. "How close have you been to the jumping-off place at the edge of the world?" he asked Ralph Bean.

"I tell you, mate, I've sailed so close to the jumping-off place I hung my foot over the edge." Ralph Bean half closed his eyes.

"What kept you from going over?"

Ralph Bean lifted his eyes in mockery. "God alone. He reached down with his great big hand and pushed the ship back on course." He winked.

Elbert pulled Peter away. "Your eyes are as big as saucers. You don't believe that nonsense, do you?"

Peter shuddered. "Not exactly, but it makes me feel creepy just the same."

"But, Peter, don't you know the world is round? I thought everybody knew that. How could there be a jumping-off place? Come on. Let's see if we can go on board."

Hours later the two ships were under way. But the *Speedwell* was in the Channel only a short while when it signaled to the *Mayflower* and turned back toward shore again.

"What's the matter? What's happened?" everyone wanted to know.

"There's a leak," the captain said.

Both ships put in at Dartmouth. Disappointment filled Peter. The new world of America had never seemed so far away. Eight days dragged by before the ships set sail again. As land was fast disappearing, Peter took a deep breath. "Now we're really on our way. Just think! This is the last we'll see of England—forever."

Two seamen went by. "This ship is still as leaky as a sieve," one remarked.

"No wonder. Look at that board. It's hardly nailed on."

The boys looked at each other. It was true. They could see water pouring through.

"The trouble is," the seaman went on, "the masts and sails are too large for the ship. Let a big blow come and it'll pull her right over. One good thing, if we sank, that busybody would keep still," and he pointed to a group of people talking in earnest tones.

Peter whispered to Elbert. "He means Christopher Martin—the one that's talking to those people. He's an Adventurer."

Christopher Martin faced the passengers. "I am treasurer of this company, and I am not accountable to you."

"But all we want to know is how we stand financially," one of the Leyden group said. "You don't have to treat us as though we weren't good enough to wipe your shoes on."

Christopher Martin snapped, "I'll handle anyone's rightful complaint, but you waspish people wouldn't be content with anything." He almost lost his footing and snarled to a passing seaman, "Don't you think we have too much sail?"

The seaman glared but said nothing. As the ship rolled, Christopher Martin and a number of others began to look green, and hurried below. Elbert looked beseechingly at Peter, then fled.

Peter's stomach moved upward several inches. He clung to the rail, not wanting to give up. Why had he ever wished to sail on a ship—any ship? With every lurch of the Speedwell, his stomach seemed ready to leap out of his mouth.

A seaman ran past shouting for the captain.

"She's sinking! She's sinking!"

For the second time both ships turned back, this time anchoring at Plymouth. Peter saw Elbert's parents, pale and shaking, drag their bundles to the deck to be taken ashore.

Peter ran to find Elbert. "Why are your parents taking everything ashore, Elbert?"

Elbert, pale from seasickness, turned his face away. "They're giving up the trip. They're going back to Leyden."

He clenched and unclenched his hands, biting his lips to keep back his tears. "I don't want to go back. I've never explained it to anyone, but I feel *called* to America. Do you know what I mean?"

"That's how I felt when I first heard of the Separatists," Peter nodded.

"To have to go back!" Elbert said. "I just can't believe it."

"Elbert, maybe Elder Brewster would take you as his second bound boy. That's how I'm listed—bound boy."

Elbert brightened and stood up, wobbling a little. The boys found the Separatist leader on deck. He agreed to take Elbert if his parents approved. Elbert's parents had hardly given their consent when the news spread that the *Speedwell* could never make the trip. It would have to be sold.

"Then we'll be on the *Mayflower!*" Peter whooped with joy.

But the following day a new problem arose.

"The *Mayflower* can't hold everybody." It was Christopher Martin speaking in his sour way. "You remember what happened to your Amsterdam friends because of overloading. More than a hundred of them died on the way to Virginia, and they had to be buried at sea. Let only immediate families go. Leave the servants behind. They can easily find employment elsewhere."

Elder Brewster protested, but Christopher Martin held firm. "I'm in charge of the finances. It is my business to see that the company makes a profit. There will be no profit if half the passengers die."

"Are bound boys servants?" Peter asked.

Christopher Martin's voice was a growl, "They certainly aren't family."

"Then—then neither Elbert nor I can go to America. We'll both have to go back to Leyden!"

Peter turned away so that Christopher Martin would not see him cry.

TRAPPED IN A SINKING SHIP

The piles of casks and crates grew high as both crew and passengers helped unload the *Speedwell*. There were the firkins of butter, kegs of flour sealed with wax, and barrels of water.

Peter stepped over some iron kettles and pointed to boxes of seed.

"Elbert, look at these." He read the labels—peas, beans, onions, parsnips, cabbage.

"I just know they'll grow twice as big in America," he said. "If only there could be some way for us to go."

Each boatload added different supplies to the growing mound—digging tools, carpenter's and mason's tools, fish nets and tackle, cloth, shoes, even blacksmith shop equipment.

"But we aren't taking any horses," Peter told Elbert,

just as if he were still going. Then he remembered, and sighed again.

Elbert comforted him. "This won't be the only trip, Peter. We'll try to go on the next one. Maybe there'll be horses then."

A number of men began to sort out supplies.

"I'll leave the fishing nets I made," one said. "I won't need them back in Leyden."

"I'm leaving this cloth I wove. They'll need it worse than I do," another said.

"Was the house brace stowed on the little ship or the big one?" a third man wanted to know.

"On the big ship. It was too long for the *Speedwell*."

Peter broke in. "Do you know how many are going back to Leyden?"

"About eighteen or twenty of us, I would say," the first man said.

"But I thought only servants had to go back. Don't you want to go to America?" Peter asked.

"Not now." The man sounded embarrassed. "This trip is not meant to take place. Look at all the trouble we've had. It's God's warning to us."

Hope sprang up in Peter's heart. He beckoned to Elbert, and they ran to find Elder Brewster.

"Everybody is going back to Leyden, Elder Brewster. There'll be plenty of room for us on the *Mayflower*," Peter said.

Elder Brewster smiled. "Now, Peter, are you sure *everybody* is going back?"

Peter felt his face grow hot. "I-I-I just mean that some people are going back."

"That's better. Yes, we have just found out that eighteen or twenty have decided not to sail." Elder Brewster

67

turned to Christopher Martin. "Wouldn't you say that's a safe margin?"

Christopher Martin growled. "Safe enough. If any more back out, we might as well all stay."

The word spread quickly: "Family servants can go after all."

"Elder Brewster, what about us? Does that mean we can go?" Peter tugged at Elder Brewster's blue coat.

"Yes, indeed, it means just that." Elder Brewster gave a hug to each boy, "Now, stay close to me. I'm going to have a roll call and you boys can help me find everyone."

Elder Brewster directed those who were returning to Leyden to stand on one side of the dock and the passengers for the *Mayflower* on the other. Peter recognized Priscilla Mullins in the *Mayflower* group, and he remembered he had not brought back her cup. In fact, he couldn't remember what happened to it. He looked around to see if John Alden had come, but he wasn't there.

Elder Brewster began roll call.

"As I call your name, please be ready to board the longboats with your family and servants. William Bradford, John Carver, Edward Winslow, Isaac Allerton, John Howland, Miles Standish, Stephen Hopkins, John Billington, Christopher Martin, William Mullins, Robert Cushman. . . ."

Robert Cushman stepped out of the group of those who were staying.

Elder Brewster looked astonished. "After all you have done to make this trip possible, aren't you going with us?"

There were tears in Robert Cushman's eyes. "No,

Elder Brewster. I have not been a well man for some weeks now. There's a weight like lead around my heart." He stood with head bowed.

Elder Brewster continued the roll call. Of the one hundred and two passengers for the *Mayflower*, thirty-three came from Leyden, sixty-seven from various parts of England, and only two from Scrooby itself—Elder Brewster and William Bradford.

Peter and Elbert counted the number of boys and girls.

"I counted thirty-eight," Peter said. "How many did you count?"

"Oh, I missed that one." Peter dashed after a two-year-old boy, Ricky More, who had slipped away from his family and was now tottering at the top of the dock steps. Peter reached him just as he lost his balance.

"Thank you, Peter," Ricky's mother said. "If I don't keep my eye on him every minute, he's gone."

The child laughed and pressed his face in his mother's skirts.

As the seamen rowed passengers to the *Mayflower*, Peter nudged Elbert and pointed out a woman who had hidden a lilac bush under her shawl. A gust of wind flipped the shawl loose, and the woman looked around defiantly as she drew the shawl tight again. Elbert pointed to a coopful of downy chicks in the arms of another woman. They both laughed to see another carrying a cat in a basket.

Elder Brewster and his family, along with Peter and Elbert, climbed into the longboat on its last trip. They had just pulled away when they heard a shout. A blond young man panted on the dockside, waving his arms.

"Who's that?" Elder Brewster asked.

"John Alden," Peter said.

"So that's our cooper, is it? It's too crowded to take him with us now." He cupped his hands and called, "Next trip." John Alden must have thought Elder Brewster meant the next trip of the *Mayflower*. He plunged into the water and swam to the boat, caught hold, and was towed to the *Mayflower*. People crowded the rail to watch the dripping young man come aboard.

Mrs. Mullins, Priscilla's mother, sniffed in disapproval. "Disgraceful exhibition."

Priscilla dropped her eyes and did not look up. John Alden walked past her, leaving little pools of water at each footstep. A pewter cup dangled at his belt. He darted a glance at Priscilla but said nothing as he went below to change into dry clothing and start his work of making barrels.

The sailors lifted anchor and hoisted sail. Twenty or twenty-five barefoot seamen worked at the ropes with rhythmic tugs, singing out directions.

"Haul up now! Lively there. Aho-o-o-o! Oh, haul now and again." The boatswain's singsong could be heard above the wind. "Heave away again. Heave lively now."

Peter recognized Ralph Bean at the helm, standing with feet apart, his mouth working in derision. The wind whipped the words out of his mouth, but Peter knew he was cursing.

In the days that followed it seemed to Peter that Ralph Bean was everywhere. He jeered after each of the three daily sermons and held his hands in mock prayer or sang hymns in a raucous voice, changing the words into nonsense. When he stood at the helm, he pretended to preach sermons.

Little Dicky More escaped from his mother one day

and crawled up to the top deck. The ship rolled so that the baby tumbled head over heels. Peter rescued him. Ralph Bean roared, "Let God pick up his fallen creatures. Isn't that what he is for?"

During fair weather families took turns cooking over a box of sand on deck. If Ralph Bean stood at the wheel he mocked them, and laughed when spray put out their fires. On night watch, he made so much noise that the men sleeping in the thirty-three-foot lifeboat on deck complained that they could not shut their eyes when he was around.

Ralph Bean had no patience with anyone who was weak or ill.

"This ship is overcrowded. What we need is to get rid of a few weaklings. One of these days I'll help cast the first of the dead into the sea. Why does your God make such weaklings? He ought to pick on somebody his own size."

The Separatists murmured against the blasphemy.

Ralph Bean shook his fist at the sky. "Why doesn't God strike me with a thunderbolt? That's what you'd like to see, isn't it? But look, nothing happens."

As if to confirm his words, the wind died into a dead calm. The ship drifted. The only sounds were the creaking of spars, the slap of cordage, and the thump of the rudder. At the helm Ralph Bean, without warning, doubled over with a violent cramp and could not straighten out. He had to be carried to his bunk. His curses could be heard over the ship.

Peter, always curious, hung around until the ship's physician, Dr. Giles Heale, sent him after hot water and told him to keep the sick man's blankets warm.

Ralph Bean thrashed in his bunk, moaned, and cried

out in delirium. Then he lay still and spoke in a quiet voice.

"Doctor, am I going to die?"

Peter was just bringing in a freshly warmed blanket.

"I'm not the doctor. I'll go get him."

"Doctor, tell me the truth."

"But I'm not—"

Ralph Bean's hand fastened on Peter's arm. "The truth, I say."

Peter tried to remember what the doctor had said. He could only recall the doctor shaking his head.

Ralph Bean's hand dropped. "I can read the truth on your face."

Peter started after the doctor.

"Don't go. I haven't much longer. I myself will be the first of the dead," Ralph screamed.

Some time later Elder Brewster came and gently pushed Peter away. Still later, the passengers watched in silence, as, wrapped in canvas, the form of Ralph Bean slipped over the railing and splashed into the sea. It was God's judgment, everyone agreed.

When the wind started to blow again the mild weather turned cold. Spray soaked the decks. Water leaked through on the triple-tiered bunks. For days no one was ever quite warm enough, and never dry.

The *Mayflower* pitched, rolled, and corkscrewed. Sometimes it lurched upward. Against orders, Peter and Elbert came up on deck to see what a storm was like.

"Go below," Captain Jones bellowed to a young man named John Howland, who staggered from handhold to handhold on the deck. The next minute a huge wave poised high above the deck and broke. Both boys cried out in horror as they saw John Howland disappear into the sea beyond.

"Look! There he is." Peter grabbed Elbert's arm.

John Howland rode the waves. He had caught hold of the topsail halyards trailing in the water. The seamen hauled him aboard with a boat hook. The boys scurried out of the way as the seamen carried him coughing and gasping to his bunk.

The storm continued. Peter and Elbert stayed in the hold with the others. The *Mayflower* pitched and bucked like a wild thing, then all but stopped as a shuddering jar shook every timber of the ship.

"She's split in two—she's breaking up! We'll sink like stone."

Shouts and footsteps sounded in the passageway.

Christopher Martin, who had come into the hold to check supplies, stared at the bulkhead.

"Look at that," he whispered, pointing to a trickle of water. As they watched, the stream widened.

Christopher Martin stumbled over his own feet. "Let's get out of here." He made his way to the hatchway. "It won't open! Something has fallen from the other side."

He began to pound with his fists. "Let me out of here, somebody! Let me out!"

A muffled voice replied, "We can't open it. The main beam has cracked amidships and one part is jammed against the hatch."

At every roll of the ship, water spurted through.

"The leak is from the top. We'll drown like rats." In his frenzy Christopher Martin clawed at the hatchway.

Water gushed in.

Peter and Elbert crowded to one side with the others and watched in silence.

"Start praying, why don't you?" Christopher Martin raged. "Don't you understand? We're going to drown, all of us."

Chapter Eight

ARROW OF DEATH

Captain Jones' voice rang out above the clamor on the other side of the jammed hatchway.

"All hands on deck! Port watch for'ard to get the spritsail off her, and then to the fore! Starboard watch take in the main. We'll lie ahull."

As soon as the *Mayflower* lay ahull, she stopped pitching; and tossing and wallowed gently in the troughs of the waves.

The passengers below could not keep their eyes off the sloshing water that washed down through the cracked mast. They moved chests and casks as far away as possible and watched the tiny waves spurt over their feet.

Someone pounded on other parts of the ship to see if there was further damage. "Don't be alarmed," Captain

Jones said. "The ship is seaworthy underneath. We're crippled, but we won't sink."

One of the Leyden group called out, "Use the house brace."

"What did you say?"

"Use the iron screw! Jack up the broken part with the iron screw."

The word passed to others outside. "The iron screw! Get the iron screw!"

The screw was dragged into place.

"Seat it on the keelson. Now, heave ho! Heave again." The men heaved in rhythm as Captain Jones chanted.

The splintered mast quivered. The men grunted with strain as they pulled and wrenched on the iron screw.

At last the passageway was opened, and Christopher Martin was the first one out.

The storm had lessened.

"Captain, how much sail?" a seaman asked.

"All she can take, but don't overpress her."

Seamen climbed aloft to shake out the furled fore topsail. Within a few minutes it was plain that the crippled mast could not bear full sail.

"Aloft and furl," the captain ordered.

There were mutters from the seamen as they smothered the sail and tied it into a neat roll. They glanced at the passengers with sulky looks.

The boatswain jerked a thumb toward the mainmast. "The upper works are leaky. One more mishap like that and—" He pointed downward.

Another seaman looked slyly at the captain. "All we need is the will to do it and we could head this ship back toward England."

Christopher Martin appeared on deck. "I want to know what's going on down there now? I've got many accounts to do, and I can't do them up here. What's the matter with those women?"

Peter, always curious, darted below to find out. Mrs. Brewster met him in the passageway and shooed him out with a flap of her apron. Her sleeves were rolled to the elbows, and she bustled about with a determined air that discouraged questions.

"No one is allowed down here now, Peter," she said.

"But why not?" Peter tried to peer beyond her.

"You'll know pretty soon. Now, run along. Oh, yes. You can do one thing for me. Find Stephen Hopkins and tell him everything is coming along as well as can be expected."

Peter found Stephen Hopkins at the rail with his head in his hands. When Peter spoke, he jumped.

""Yes, yes, Peter. What is it? Has anything happened?"

"No, sir. I mean, I don't know, sir. Mrs. Brewster says everything is coming along as well as can be expected, whatever that means."

Stephen Hopkins let out a sigh that was half groan. "If I could only do something instead of standing around here helpless."

"Is someone sick, sir?"

"No. Oh, no. Not sick. I don't think you could call it sick. The Bible speaks of it. It's a natural process." He wiped the perspiration off his forehead and gripped the railing. "It's perfectly natural, but I can't get used to it."

Not long after, Mrs. Brewster, face aglow, rushed along the deck. "It's a boy! It's a boy!"

Stephen Hopkins burst into tears, pumped Mrs. Brewster's hand, and plunged down the hatchway, followed by the cheers of everyone on deck.

Tiny Oceanus Hopkins lay in the only cradle brought on the *Mayflower*. He was the first newborn baby Peter had ever seen.

"He's so little and—and shriveled," Peter told Elbert. "How long will he be like that?"

Elbert laughed. "By the time we reach land, he'll probably be able to walk off the ship by himself."

But Oceanus had hardly grown at all when the longed for word was cried at last. "Land! Land, ho!"

The passengers crowded to the rail. They talked, prayed, and wept for joy. It took some time before Captain Jones found a safe harbor. Christopher Martin grumbled because everyone hung over the railing for such long periods of time.

"Don't you people realize we have to elect a governor, learn to use the muskets, and mend the shallop [a shallop is a large rowboat]? It's just about ruined from so many sleeping in it."

Elder Brewster soothed him. "Patience, patience. Everything in its season."

John Carver was elected governor and he helped draw up a compact for government in the new colony. The majority signed it.

Captain Standish taught the Separatists how to use a musket. Peter and the other boys helped by holding the musket rest, a pointed staff with forked head. Being both quick and steady, Peter won praise from Captain Standish.

"We'll take you on the first exploring party," he promised. "After that, each boy in turn can go."

Peter ran to find John Alden. "How long before you have the shallop mended?"

John Alden shook his head. "Many days, I fear."

Now the women began to clamor. "Can't we go ashore in the small boats? We must wash clothes."

On the first good day, they landed with wooden washtubs, iron kettles, and square mallets to pound the clothes clean. The men built fires and heated fresh water from nearby streams. The women sang as they worked, even though their wet skirts froze in the wind.

More than two weeks afterward, small boats carried sixteen or twenty men wearing corselets and carrying muskets on the first trip of exploration. Peter wore a cloth jerkin interwoven with wire under his padded coat. When he first walked on land, his legs trembled, and it seemed to him the earth was weaving under his feet.

The air was cold. There were traces of snow. The men kept a sharp lookout for signs of other human beings. No one knew what to expect.

"Fresh footprints!"

A chill of fear passed through Peter.

"There's someone ahead of us!"

Peter caught a glimpse of a back disappearing into the depths of the woods.

"Follow him, men!" Captain Standish plunged into the underbrush. Briars and thickets slowed down the exploring party.

"We've lost the tracks."

Peter felt both disappointed and relieved. After a wakeful night huddled around a fire, the party started out the next day. They came across heaps of sand.

"Look!" William Bradford pointed. "What are these mounds? There must be hundreds."

The men dug into one and unearthed first a painted

board. Under a mat they found bowls, trays, and dishes. Two bundles, one large and one small, lay under these. In the large one they found a knife, a pack needle, two or three iron kettles, a pair of fringed deerskin trousers, and a packet of red powder. A strong but not offensive smell came from the excavation.

William Bradford knocked the earth off a round object from the lame bundle. It was a skull with hair still attached.

"A grave! We have opened a grave!"

The small bundle contained the skeleton of a child. Bracelets of fine white beads circled the leg bones. A little bow had been placed by his side.

"Put these back and dig no more." Elder Brewster spoke quietly. "We cannot desecrate the dead."

Captain Standish examined the site. "They must have had a war or disease, perhaps plague."

Another member of the party, John Billington, ran up. "I've just found their grain field."

Stephen Hopkins called, "I've found where they've had a house. There are planks and a big kettle and mounds of earth."

"We will not touch those," Elder Brewster said.

"These aren't graves, I'm sure."

Two brothers, John and Edward Tillery, began to dig into some mounds.

"It's a basket." They tugged at a woven container, narrow at the top and swelling out. It was filled with three or four bushels of a squarish grain, some deep yellow, others red and blue.

Captain Standish took up a handful. "This must be the Indian corn we've heard about in England."

The men dug up a number of baskets.

"There's enough corn to feed us for a long time. Shall we take it, Elder Brewster?"

"Yes." Elder Brewster picked up some corn and let it run from one hand to the other. "It's clear that the Indians have deserted this place. Let us take the corn, for it may save our lives, but let us vow to repay these people if we should ever meet them."

The men brought back the corn to the *Mayflower*. It was examined with curiosity and gratitude, and stored for seed.

By the time it was Peter's turn again to go on an exploring trip, the weather was bitterly cold. Spray froze on the men's coats, making a glaze of ice. Peter shivered as an icy gale hit the shallop. He was glad to help dig for more corn on land. The men found about ten bushels, all in all.

That night they made a barricade of logs and boughs, and appointed a sentinel.

"Smoke! There's smoke down the beach," the sentinel called not long after.

It could only mean Indians.

"We won't stir from here tonight," Captain Standish said. He divided the party into two groups, one to explore by land and one by shallop. Peter was in the land party. The next morning they found the campsite of the previous night.

"They've been cutting up a big fish." Captain Standish pointed out piles of fat about two inches thick. Several pieces of the fish lay on the beach.

During the rest of the day, no one caught so much as a glimpse of another human being. At sundown, the land party met the shallop at a creek.

The men cut logs, stakes, and thick pine boughs for a

barricade, leaving one side open and making a fire in the middle. They lay around the fire, with a sentinel on guard. Peter tucked himself in between Elder Brewster and William Bradford.

A hideous cry brought Peter to his feet out of a sound sleep.

"Arm yourselves, men!" the sentinel shouted. The men scrambled for their muskets and shot out into the cold night. The noise ceased.

"So that's what Indians sound like." Peter huddled close to the others.

"Not Indians, but wolves," a seaman with the party explained. "I've been around this country before up in Newfoundland, and I've heard them often."

"Then what do Indians sound like?" Peter wanted to know, but none of the men could tell him.

Peter was up with the rest when the tide came in at five the next morning.

After prayer and breakfast, the men prepared to break camp and load the shallop.

"Shall we take the muskets down first or last?" someone asked. He unwrapped his musket and wiped off the dew.

Some said to leave them. Others protested, "No, we'd better have them with us. Who knows? Perhaps we're being watched this very minute. We can't take chances."

Some left their muskets in camp and some took theirs to the shallop.

A weird, strange cry, high and foreboding, pierced the early morning air.

"Woach! Woach! Ha! Ha! Hach! Woach!"

Peter knew that this was no wolf. The cry rang out again. The eerie sound made Peter's flesh crawl. Something moved at the edge of the forest.

"Indians! Men, it's Indians!"

Something whizzed by Peter and thudded into the pine stake behind him. He heard another, and another.

Some of the men ran to get their muskets from the shallop. Those at the barricade worked with feverish haste getting into armor and loading the four remaining muskets.

Captain Standish alone remained calm. "Don't fire until I give the word."

It was just daylight, and Peter got his first good look at Indians.

Their long black braids flopped against their backs as they ran. Bright feathers bobbed upright. Their faces were hideously streaked with red and black paint, and the whites of their eyes gleaned.

Yelling their horrid chant, the Indians darted from tree to tree, fitting arrows to their bows at a run.

Those arrows meant death.

A soft slithering sound made Peter turn. He saw two bright feathers before he saw the streaked face of an Indian, peering from behind a tree. Before Peter could yell a warning, he heard a mighty whir, felt himself flung against a pine stake and pinned there by an arrow still quivering with the impact. It had caught his coat through the heavy padding just above the shoulder.

Peter tried to wriggle free, but could not. He pulled at the arrow with both hands. It did not budge. He gasped in horror and tried to call for help, but his mouth was so dry he could not make a sound. Blood pounded in his eardrums as he saw the Indian with a deft movement draw another arrow and aim straight at his heart.

UP IN SMOKE

.

Peter hunched his shoulders and half turned to ward off the arrow. As in a dream, he heard Miles Standish's voice.

"Fire!"

For one dizzying second Peter thought Miles Standish had ordered the Indian to shoot. Then the world exploded. The roar of the gunshot rang in Peter's ears as he looked back. The Indian stood frozen with fright. He had dropped his bow and arrow. Bits of bark and leaves rained around him.

Two more shots exploded. The Indian shrieked and bounded into the woods. His companions melted into the forest without a sound.

Captain Standish brandished his musket. "After them, men! Show them we are not afraid."

Metal rattled against metal as the men in their armor crashed through the underbrush. Peter heard one or two more shots, and then the men came back.

"No one can run through the woods with all this on," William Bradford said as he took off his corselet and helmet. "I don't think they'll be back."

Peter still struggled to free himself. Elder Brewster ran to help. The others crowded around with exclamations of concern. Elder Brewster braced his foot against the stake and wrenched the arrow out.

Peter flopped down. His legs trembled.

"Are you hurt, Peter?" Elder Brewster asked as he examined Peter's shoulder.

"No, sir, but I'd like to sit here for a few minutes."

He watched the men pick up their coats, which they had tossed on the barricade. There were exclamations of disbelief. The coats had been shot through and through by arrows.

Some of the arrowheads were tipped with the claws of a large bird honed to a sharp edge. Others were made of horn, bone, or flint. The men collected eighteen and gave them to Peter to take back to the *Mayflower*.

The exploring party set out in the boat to find a place where they could make a colony. Peter kept looking at the arrow that had almost killed him.

"Will we have Indian attacks like this all the time?"

Second Mate Robert Coppin, who had been in the new land on other trips, reassured him. "Not if we make a treaty with the Indians. But I know a spot around here someplace that ought to be quite protected." He scrutinized the coastline until rain blurred it from sight. The wind increased.

There was a cry of dismay from the steersman.

"There goes the rudder. It broke clean off."

Peter looked back and saw the rudder whirl to the top of the water and disappear.

Two men grabbed oars and tried to guide the boat. The shallop bounced like a cork. The masts creaked under the strain of the sails.

Second Mate Robert Coppin shouted a warning. "Lie low! The mast is cracking. Look to your lives!"

A piece of the mast crashed near Peter. The collaps-

ing sail enveloped him. He tried to thrash his way clear.

"It's broken in three pieces," he heard someone call. Peter felt himself rolled over and over. He dug with his hands and feet to keep from going overboard. The sail skimmed over his back and landed in the sea.

"To the harbor! To the harbor!" Robert Coppin kept repeating. "This is the place." Then, as the full sea lifted the shallop high on the waves, he let out a groan. "Lord, be merciful unto me. My eyes have never seen this place before."

The shallop was being tossed toward a cove full of breakers.

"About with her, or we are all cast away." Robert Coppin made a violent circling motion with his hand. "Row lustily."

A rocky promontory loomed before them. It looked as though the shallop would splinter to pieces on it.

Unexpectedly, the churning waters turned calm. The men lay on the lee side, panting and shivering in the relative quiet.

"We'll have to stay on the shallop tonight," someone said. "The Indians won't attack us here."

Another argued, "No, we'll have to go ashore and get a fire going. We'll freeze to death in these wet clothes."

"But we can't have a fire. It will attract the Indians."

It was decided to go ashore but not make a fire. Peter shivered with the others all night long, sleeping fitfully.

The next day the sun shone. The wind had shifted. Captain Standish appeared puzzled that there were no signs of life. Then he made a discovery.

"We're safe. This is an island."

In high spirits the men built a roaring fire, dried their clothes, fixed their muskets, and rested. The next

87

day was Sunday. They spent the day in prayer and singing. Elder Brewster preached. In his final prayer he sought God's guidance for the exploring party in finding a place to live.

The next morning the shallop had hardly skirted the bay when Captain Standish pointed in excitement to a slope rising out of the harbor. "That's the place we want."

Elder Brewster sounded doubtful. "It looks rather barren."

A plateau rose about thirty feet above the edge of the sea and sloped up to a hill about 150 feet high.

"We need a hill like that for a lookout." Captain Standish kept on until he won his point.

Peter looked around in amazement. "But there isn't anything here."

The others laughed and teased him. "Did you expect to find houses already waiting for us, Peter?"

Peter saw only sandy waste, a few rocks and shrubs, a hill, and a stream of water, with a fringe of woods.

Elder Brewster pointed out the good black earth, wild fruit trees, herbs, and berries, as well as fine clay. "It will wash pots and pans like soap. A most hopeful place to live," he said.

Captain Standish hurried the men to the woods to explore farther back. Peter, near the end of the single file, heard a shout and hurried to see what was happening.

"I tell you, it's a deer trap." Stephen Hopkins pointed to saplings lined up in an oblong. A thick pole leaned at an angle. Acorns littered the ground.

"What's a deer trap?" William Bradford came around to look. As he crossed the trail, a sapling jerked upward, a hidden noose caught him by the leg and swung him in the air by one heel. He grabbed at the sapling but could not reach it. The others bent down the sapling and loosened the Indian rope.

"I'm glad it didn't catch me by the neck." William Bradford rubbed his leg and examined the rope with the others. It was strong and pliable.

The men teased William Bradford all the way back to the *Mayflower*. "We'll make you chief scout for deer traps," they said.

Peter ran to find Elbert, who lay ill in one of the triple-tiered bunks.

"You'll have to hurry and get over whatever it is you have, Elbert. There's so much to see and do." Peter described every detail of the exploring trip. "You don't want to miss your turn."

Elbert's eyes shone bright with fever. "A lot of people are sick, Peter. Most of the women are. Do you remember how their skirts froze the day they washed clothes?"

Peter remembered. When he came to see Elbert again, he had more news. "About half the crew is sick. Dr. Heale says it's scurvy. He says I can help him."

Calls came from every part of the ship. Dr. Heale and Deacon Fuller took charge. Even with help from those who were well, the two men could not care for all the sick.

The crew would not help one another.

"No—no—I'm not going to risk death. Let him look after himself," the gunner said when the boatswain was taken ill. The gunner became ill himself, and Mrs. Brewster nursed him.

The gunner began to weep. "I see you show your love like Christians, one to another. We let one another lie and die like dogs."

In spite of sickness, the men who were able to do so went ashore every day for weeks to chop trees, strip off branches, cut thatch, and build huts and the Common House. Some days rain, sleet, and wind prevented work. Nevertheless, the barricade, two sheds, a hospital, and several shelter huts took shape.

Peter was proud to guide Dr. Heale on his first trip ashore. They walked along the street, or First Street, as some called it.

This street ran almost eight hundred feet from the water's edge to the top of Fort Hill. Two men ran onto the street from the side of an unfinished hut. Peter recognized the two Edwards, Edward Doty and Edward Leister, servants of Stephen Hopkins.

"What are they doing?" Peter gasped.

Edward Doty attacked the other Edward with a sword. Edward Leister defended himself with a dagger, dropped it, and clutched his arm. Blood seeped through his fingers.

Their shouts brought others to the place where the two men stood glaring at each other. Elder Brewster grabbed Edward Doty by his jerkin.

"What do you mean by dueling, disabling yourselves like this?"

Both men had wounds.

"Have you forgotten the purpose for which we have all worked, suffered, even died?" Elder Brewster shook the man.

"But he's been using my tools every day and he never asks permission," Edward Doty said.

"I don't use them all the time—I just wanted to smooth the mud when it's wet," the other Edward replied.

Elder Brewster appealed to Governor Carver. "What do you think about this?"

Governor Carver reflected and spoke in his slow way.

"We don't have any stocks, or I'd have you both in them to think over your problems."

The two men hung their heads. "It won't happen again," they promised.

"Very well. Perhaps Deacon Fuller and Dr. Heale will dress your wounds."

Deacon Fuller bound up the gash in Edward Leister's arm, and Dr. Heale bandaged Edward Doty's side.

Afterward, Peter pointed out the lots on each side of the street as he continued to act as Dr. Heale's guide.

"There are to be nineteen family lots."

"But, Peter, where will the unmarried men live?"

"They choose the family they want," Peter explained. He showed Dr. Heale the partly built hut of the Brewsters. "I live here. You can see the kitchen and living room. There's a ladder to the sleeping platform." Peter waved at the empty air and saw Dr. Heale smile. "You'll see, Dr. Heale. It will soon be finished."

At the Common House, Peter showed Dr. Heale the supplies stacked inside. Loaded muskets lay in the corner. A blast of wind whistled through the chinks in the wall.

"The wind and rain strip the mud off." Peter showed how mud had been plastered between the logs.

A man called Dr. Heale's name. "Oh, doctor," he said as he came in, "Deacon Fuller would like to see you."

Peter went with Dr. Heale to the hospital hut. A man lay wrapped in blankets.

Deacon Fuller talked in a low voice. "He spent last night on the bare ground—got lost hunting for thatch. His feet are frozen."

"Any hope, Dr. Heale?" Deacon Fuller asked when they were outside.

"None. There is nothing we can do."

Later, after the man died, Captain Standish gave strict orders. "The grave must be leveled out like all the other graves. The Indians must not know how many have died."

Peter well knew by now that life in the New World was a desperate affair.

After the service, many went back to the *Mayflower*. At six o'clock the next morning Peter heard the lookout shouting in alarm, "Fire! Fire ashore!"

People hurried to the deck.

"Where is it?"

"It looks like—but it can't be—yes, it is—it's the Common House."

There was a groan of dismay.

"To the boats—to the boats!"

"No, we can't. It's low tide."

The men stared white-faced. It was not necessary to say what a fire would mean.

Sometimes the strong wind flattened out the flame and smoke on shore. Then it would leap up afresh. The minute the tide turned, the men leaped into the boats and headed toward shore.

Peter clung to the rail. "Will they make it? Will they get there in time?"

A gust of wind shot a shower of sparks off the Common House roof.

Christopher Martin finally said what no one wanted to hear.

"When the fire reaches the loaded muskets . . . ." He lifted his hands in a swift, upward movement.

Peter watched with the others, helpless and silent, waiting for the explosion that would destroy the Common House, tools, weapons, and most important of all, the precious seed that meant their very lives.

TOO MANY GUESTS

Christoper Martin joined the lookout on the forecastle. He paced back and forth, complaining at every step.

"How am I ever going to straighten out any accounts, with everything destroyed by fire?" He appeared to be talking to himself.

"But look!" Peter shouted. "The blaze is dying out."

Christopher Martin shook his head. "I don't think so. It has only dropped inside."

When the folks on the land started back to the ship, Christopher Martin complained again. "Are they going to leave everything to the fire?"

The men in the boats waved cheerfully as they approached the *Mayflower*.

"God granted us a miracle," they said in describing the blaze. "Only the thatch burned."

The morning service included special thanksgiving for the act of Providence that had spared the Common House.

Peter helped Elbert to the deck afterward. The lookout stopped them.

"Tell me something." He looked around to see whether anyone could overhear. "The thatch roof burned, didn't it?"

"Yes, sir, it did."

"It needs fixing, doesn't it?"

"Oh, yes. It will have to be renewed entirely."

"Then why are all the men here on board?"

"It's the Sabbath."

"What difference does that make? Why aren't they on shore fixing that roof?"

"Well—" Peter could not think of an answer. Elbert straightened his thin shoulders and spoke with heat. "We don't work on the Sabbath. That's the day we give to God."

The lookout stared, then went on his way, shaking his head.

In the next few weeks building was often interrupted by a sad task—the digging of graves. One was for Christopher Martin, who fretted to the last about his accounts. Priscilla Mullins' parents died, and she came to live with the Brewsters. There was a grave, too, for Elbert Farham, who slipped away with a smile for Peter. "I'm tired, very tired, Peter," he said as he died.

In his first grief over the loss of his friend, Peter let the tears flow, but he knew that weeping would not help with the many difficulties that faced the settlers, so he dried his eyes and went to do his share with the others.

One of his jobs was to help the men strip branches

from the trees they had cut. One morning he found a branch hard to manage. He flung it aside, but it bounced back. Irritated, Peter took it in both arms to the edge of the trail and kicked it. But he caught his toe in it and fell backward against someone standing behind him.

"Excuse me," he began, turning to apologize. The words died on his lips. An Indian, almost naked except for a leather girdle, stood holding a bow. Streaks of black and red paint covered his cheeks and forehead. Two feathers stuck out of his black hair. He stared over Peter's head as if Peter weren't there.

"Elder Brewster!" Peter's half-strangled gasp jerked the men to attention. They stopped in the act of chopping down trees. Others let the logs they were dragging slip to the ground.

The muskets lay out of reach.

The Indian stepped forward. "Wel-come, Englishmen. Wel-come, Englishmen!"

With a sigh of relief Elder Brewster stepped forward, his hand outstretched. The Indian bowed his head in acknowledgment.

"You live in Pawtuxet?" The Indian pointed.

"Yes. Did you used to live here? We owe you for some corn we took, and . . . ."

"Yes, I was born in Pawtuxet. Now I am almost the only one left. Four years ago the Great Spirit sent a plague that wiped out almost the whole tribe. No one will come back. You can live here if you wish."

"Come and see it." Elder Brewster beckoned the Indian to the trail. Peter followed close enough to hear.

Elder Brewster stopped as if he had suddenly thought of something. "But where did you learn to speak English? And what is your name?"

"My name is Samoset. I am chief of the Pemaquid tribe. I learned English from the fishermen."

"Are any of your people with you?"

Samoset shook his head. "I am alone. But I'll bring some of my people. One of them has been to England."

Five days later Samoset returned with several Indians, all wearing deerskin capes, except for one who wore wildcat skin. The Indians showed curiosity in everything the settlers were doing. They fingered their clothes, rubbed their fingers over the oiled-linen windowpanes, and ran their hands over the logs. They ate biscuits, butter, cheese, pudding. When Governor Carver gave them gifts of knives, bracelets, and rings their impassive faces broke into delighted smiles. They nodded and bowed as they made their way into the forest.

The next day Samoset reappeared with another Indian. Peter knew at once that this plan was different.

"This is Squanto," Samoset said.

Squanto was tall and dark-eyed like Samoset. But where Samoset was almost dishfaced, Squanto had high cheekbones, a broad brow, and a wide mouth. Peter liked him.

Squanto adopted the settlers at once. Every day he emerged from the woods and helped the men at whatever task they were working on. Peter was at his heels all day.

In the next few weeks Squanto showed how to tap maple trees, how to make fishhooks of bone, how to squeeze the eels from their mud burrows with his feet, how to fell trees by plastering damp clay above and below a strip and then burning through the strip. When it was time to plant corn, Squanto grub-hoed with everyone else.

After many days of backbreaking work, Peter straightened up and surveyed the field. "We must have dug a hundred thousand holes. Isn't it time to put the grain in, Squanto?"

Squanto shook his head. "Not until the oak leaves are as big as a mouse's ear. Besides, there is no food for the corn to eat."

"But, Squanto, corn doesn't eat."

"Corn eats fish." Squanto taught the men to put three small fish crisscross at the bottom of each hole. He showed the women how to weave willow baskets for carrying fish.

"Now the corn can eat," he said.

At night around the hearth fire Squanto told how white men had captured him and his companions and taken them to England. Every time he used the words "white man," Squanto drew his fingers across his forehead.

Peter imitated. "Why does that mean 'white man'?"

"It stands for their broad-brimmed hats."

This was the first of a number of meanings in sign language that Peter learned from Squanto.

"How did you get back here, Squanto?"

"The white men needed a guide when they came back to trade. I am Chief Massasoit's interpreter."

"Who is Chief Massasoit?"

"He is chief over seven tribes." Squanto waved his hand to include the whole territory. "Massasoit is a big, big man."

Squanto was a tall man himself, and Peter expected to see a giant when Chief Massasoit came to visit later.

He was tall, but no taller than his men. Chief Massasoit wore a deerskin over one shoulder, a chain of white bone beads, and a leather tobacco pouch. A long knife swung by a cord around his neck.

Sixty Indians clustered behind him. Some had black streaks painted on their faces; others had red, yellow, or white. Many had furs. All were well built.

Squanto acted as interpreter.

"This is Chief Massasoit."

Governor Carver and Chief Massasoit kissed each other's hands.

"Chief Massasoit has come in peace."

After a few words of greeting, Chief Massasoit withdrew with great dignity. When he came the next time he stood on a neighboring hill with four of his men. They came no closer.

Governor Carver called for Squanto. "What does he want?"

Squanto sped back with the message. "Chief Massasoit has come to parley."

Governor Carver spoke to Edward Window. "Go greet him."

In a few minutes Winslow returned. "He wants to buy my sword and armor, for one thing."

"We can't sell those."

The next visit Chief Massasoit crossed the brook, followed by twenty of his Wampanoag followers. They left their bows and arrows behind them. Miles Standish with six armed men went to meet them, and laid down their armor and muskets. Captain Standish then ushered Chief Massasoit to Elder Brewster's house. A green rug was spread on the floor and several cushions put down. As Chief Massasoit entered, there was a sound of trumpet and drum. The Indian guests appeared impressed.

Through Squanto, Chief Massasoit made the purpose of his visit known.

"Neither I, Chief Massasoit, nor my people will hurt any of the colonists."

Governor Carver nodded.

"If any of my people do, they will be sent to Pawtuxet for punishment by the Englishmen."

Again Governor Carver nodded.

"If an Englishman offends Chief Massasoit or his people, he shall be sent to me for punishment. That is just, is it not, Governor Carver?"

"Yes."

"And if anything is stolen, it will be restored, on either side."

"Agreed."

"If there is an unjust war against the colonists, I, Chief Massasoit, will aid you."

"We thank you," Governor Carver said.

"And if there is unjust war against Massasoit, you will help."

"Yes."

"When visiting each other, all arms will be left behind."

Governor Carver looked to Captain Standish, who nodded.

"Englishmen, take possession of the land. There is no one left to occupy it. The Great Spirit came in his anger and swept our people from the face of the earth. I give this land to you and your people forever."

Governor Carver gave a copper chain with a jewel in it to Chief Massasoit, and gifts of knives to the Indians.

Some of the Indians tried to blow the trumpet. Their red cheeks puffed out and grew purple with effort as they tried to force air through the metal tube. Much to the merriment of the others, no one could produce more than a squawk. As they filed out, one tried to take the trumpet with him. Captain Standish retrieved it with a smile.

The lookout ran in a few minutes later.

"Their women and children have come to camp. They walked forty miles in one day."

The next morning Governor Carver gave Chief Massasoit a parting gift of a large kettle filled with dry peas.

Squanto reported that the chief was well pleased, and said that the Great Spirit would smile upon the new people who now lived on the land where so many had died.

In the middle of the next week Governor Carver complained of a headache while working in the cornfield. He died a few days later.

"Your chief is gone. Will your people move away?" Squanto asked.

The new governor, William Bradford, tried to explain. "No, we shall not move. Our Great Spirit bids us keep on no matter what the difficulties or sorrow. He will reward us in time."

Squanto was satisfied.

The lookout ran down with a warning. "Forty Indians are coming."

The women, with little cries, ran to prepare food for the visitors. The Indians went away content. A few days later ten from another tribe appeared. A week after that a party of eighteen hunters brought game to be roasted.

Peter listened to the worried talk among the women. "Yes, it's true they bring meat, but that doesn't happen every time. Our other supplies are running low. And we haven't had rain for several weeks. The situation is growing serious."

The corn wilted. Everyone watched the sky, but there was no sign of rain. Still, every time Indian guests came, they were fed.

Governor Bradford called for a day of fasting and prayer. No one left the church except the guards, who took turns as lookout on the flat roof overhead.

The heat inside was stifling. In the evening on the way down the hill, no one spoke.

Peter climbed up to the sleeping platform. Below, Elder Brewster talked with his wife.

"We must cut the food ration by half tomorrow."

"But, William, people are already faint from the fast."

"Yes, but if we are going to live at all, we must be satisfied to be a little bit hungry."

Peter lay on one side and then the other. He twisted and turned, and finally lay on his stomach to still his hunger pangs. It seemed to him that he had been hungry all his life.

Chapter Eleven

THE SNAKESKIN TALKS

Peter Cook woke with a start. For a minute he thought he was on the *Mayflower* again, dipping and sinking with the roll of the ship. But that was seven months ago.

He heard the rustle of his cornhusk mattress, the scrape of a spoon against an iron kettle, and the snap and whoosh of flames in the fireplace. He knew where he was now—at Pawtuxet, the day after the fast.

A strange rumble, like drums, throbbed far away. Indians! Peter's heart thumped. It couldn't be Squanto. He never came with a drum. Squanto came in silence, his tall figure unmoving, his black eyes alert, his wide mouth almost smiling. Peter made himself lie still and listen, the way Squanto had taught him.

The sound that woke Peter beat like waves on his eardrums, but it was different from the murmur of the sea. It was more like a feeling. It quivered under his narrow sleeping platform.

He sat up, frightened. He opened his mouth to call Mrs. Brewster, then discovered that the distant surging was not an outside noise at all. It was inside him; in fact, in his stomach,

Peter was hungry. He had not eaten for thirty-six hours.

He remembered the day before, when he sat with the others under the low-beamed ceiling of the church on the hill, fasting and praying for rain to break the six-weeks' dry spell and save the corn crop. Even the guards overhead where the distant cannons pointed their snouts in four directions had fasted.

But today Peter could eat. He smelled something good, and dressed in a hurry. He gasped as he climbed down from his sleeping platform and saw full daylight spill through the open doorway. The oiled-linen windowpane steamed from the hot sun. He checked the noon mark on the windowsill. It was already past noon.

"Mrs. Brewster, what happened? Why did you let me sleep so long?"

Mrs. Brewster turned and patted her moist face with the edge of her apron.

"I let you sleep, lad, because that way you wouldn't feel it so much." She sighed.

"Feel what, Mrs. Brewster? Fast day is over." Peter hung over the kettle sniffing the good smell clear to his toes. "Why, Mrs. Brewster, this is corn *pudding*. Is this our thanksgiving after yesterday's fast? M'mmm. I could eat the whole kettleful."

Mrs. Brewster sighed again. Then Peter remembered. There would be only half the food ration from now on.

"I'll eat my half right now," Peter said.

He ran to get his wooden trencher and spoon, but Mrs. Brewster did not look up from her stirring. "Peter, you must try to forget your hunger until our guests are served. Then you may eat."

"Guests? Who?"

"They're waiting at the Common House. Come, help me carry the kettle."

"But Mrs. Brewster, do we have to give all our food to the Indians? We fed thirty last week. Why does Chief Massasoit let them come? He knows we won't have much food left if the corn crop fails."

Mrs. Brewster lifted the kettle from the fire. "Chief Massasoit can't be everywhere. He is chief over many tribes. We must keep the Indians our friends. Do you understand? Our very lives depend on it."

"But—" Peter stopped at Mrs. Brewster's stern look and pulled in his leather belt another notch. He put on his wide brimmed hat to keep off the July sun. Without a word he helped Mrs. Brewster balance the kettle between them.

At the Common House women scurried in and out with platters of food.

One of the women hailed them. "Just in time, Mrs. Brewster. I hope this will fill them up for a month."

The Indian guests sat at a long table at the side of the Common House. Peter watched their hands reach for fish, clams, beans, and wild berries. The muscles of the Indians' backs glistened with fish oil and rippled with every move. The bright feathers in their headbands bobbed as the Indians crammed food into their mouths. Peter swayed from hunger.

One of the Indians caught up a steaming clam with

his white bone fishhook. His companions laughed, and at once everyone outdid the first. If food dropped, it was pushed off the table. Peter's eyes followed every wasted bite as it fell. He swallowed hard.

Several of the Indians loosened the leather thongs of their loincloths. Their stomachs curved out like the prow of a ship. Peter hoped they were too full to eat the pudding, but by the time each one greedily received his portion, Peter gave up hope. The kettle was empty.

The Indians poured pitchers of maple syrup over the pudding, snacked their lips, and ate as if they had fasted for days. They held the bowls high to let the last drops of maple syrup drip on their tongues. Peter could not bear to watch any longer. He had helped tap the maple trees for sugar sap. Now all the syrup was gone.

Anger churned his stomach. If Chief Massasoit knew that these braves kept visiting Pawtuxet and eating the people's food, he would tell them to bring their own. Chief Massasoit and his warriors always brought extra food. Someone ought to go and explain to him that there would be no food at all if the corn crop died because of lack of rain.

When the Indians started games of skill, target shooting, and wrestling, everyone watched. Peter took the pudding kettle into the Common House and scraped every morsel from the sides and bottom. There was just enough to make his stomach clamor for more.

"I'll go myself and tell Chief Massasoit," he said to himself.

He looked around at the supplies, trying to decide what to take on the long trip. He put on a corselet armor. It was so heavy he could not walk. He took it off and tried on a helmet. It hung over his ears. The swords were so long he tripped.

Peter made sure his own knife was in his belt and put his hat back on. At least he could carry a gift. Messengers always took presents.

He lifted the lid of a box made of birch bark. A string of beads or a copper trinket would be fine. A silvery glitter caught his eye and he gasped. A rattlesnake skin, each scale shiny, lay in the box. It was wrapped around a cluster of arrows. This was the gift an Indian had brought Governor Bradford the day before. Governor Bradford had pounded his fist on the table and roared, "I'll send a gift back myself—thunderbolts and lightning."

A rattlesnake skin must be very important, Peter decided. It wouldn't be polite to send back the same arrows. He thought a moment, undid the skin, and poured gunshot clear to the top. He fastened the skin to his belt and slipped outside.

The Indians sang and danced with spine-tingling frenzy. Clouds of dust arose as they stomped and shouted. Peter hurried down the street without looking back. The snakeskin bumped against his legs at every step. He wrapped it around his waist inside his blouse.

"I'll stay in sight of the sea," he thought, "and I'll make a barricade on the beach the way we did last winter."

All afternoon Peter trudged over the sand mounds and sparse grassy tufts. Near sundown he found a fresh water rivulet and made camp by cutting a pile of branches and twigs. He curled up near a sandy ledge and listened to the night sounds from the sea, the rustlings in the sand around him, and the stirrings in the forest.

His own heartbeat drowned out other sounds until he remembered that Squanto told him every Indian boy

Peter's age went out alone just the way he was doing, to prove himself a man. Peter said his prayers and fell asleep.

Loud voices waked him. It was daylight. A circle of painted Indians bent over him.

"Owanux! Owanux!" they called, pointing toward Pawtuxet. Peter knew they meant *Englishmen.*

"Massasoit! Massasoit!" he said, pointing in the opposite direction. He remembered Squanto's sign for chief, and pointed up, raising his right hand above his face and tracing an arc. "One who stands above his people," Squanto had explained.

Peter stood up and the snakeskin gave way. Balls of shot rolled around his waist. He drew out the skin and began putting the shot into the snake's mouth. There was an intake of breath. The Indians stepped back muttering. Peter fastened the skin on the outside of his waist. Every eye was on him. No one made a move toward him.

"Massasoit!" Peter said. A brave beckoned to him and pointed out one of the birch canoes on the beach. As Peter stepped in, a faint roll of thunder rumbled in the distance. The Indians looked at one another.

The canoes skimmed the water. The arms of the braves were as straight as their paddles. One of them pointed to the sky. Massed clouds rimmed the horizon.

After a long trip the Indians escorted Peter to their camp. The women shrank back and shielded their children behind skirts of smoked skins. Peter walked straight to a grill where fish broiled over coals. He made the sign of hunger, a back-and-forth movement of his open hand, palm up, across his stomach.

One of the braves pushed a woman forward. With

many uneasy looks at Peter, she put food in a burned-clay bowl and set it before him. He ate until he had to loosen his belt three notches. With a sigh of content, he moved his cupped right hand up and down to indicate enough. Some of the women giggled, covering their mouths with their hands.

When night fell, a woman pointed out a hut, a long wooden frame covered with woven cane. The walls were plastered clay. Peter stretched out on a mat placed on a pile of fragrant boughs. Then he sat up. For the first tine he realized he could not talk to Chief Massasoit without an interpreter. Peter knew only a few Indian words and signs.

In the morning he ate as much as he had the night before. He kept asking, "Squanto?" to the Indians who crept out to stare at him. They shook their heads.

A murmur like a forest breeze came to Peter's ears. Raindrops splattered on his hand. Someone pointed to the woods and grunted a name. It passed from one Indian to another. A tall Indian stepped out.

"Squanto!" Peter rushed to meet him. Squanto's eyes were unsmiling as he looked from Peter to the Indians. He caught Peter by the shoulder.

"What are you doing here, Peter?"

Squanto looked so angry, Peter chose his words carefully.

"I'm a messenger."

"Messenger? Why would the Englishmen send a boy as a messenger? Do they mock their enemies by sending an unarmed boy?"

"Oh no, Squanto. They didn't send me. I—I mean, I'm a messenger, all right, only I sent myself."

"What do you mean by that?"

"I came to tell Chief Massasoit not to let his braves eat up all our food."

"But, Peter, this is not Massasoit's camp. Massasoit is many miles away." Squanto pointed. "I come from Massasoit as messenger myself. This tribe has disobeyed Massasoit for a long time. He has sent the war challenge."

Squanto held up a rattlesnake skin stuffed with arrows.

Peter's breath was suddenly gone. "War! Does that mean war?" Peter made sure that his snakeskin did not show.

"Yes. Already they are preparing." Squanto turned Peter toward camp. "See?"

Some of the Indians were painting their faces with jagged stripes of black, white, and yellow. Others laid out arrows, testing the tips. Still others restrung their largest bows. Someone started a weird chant low in his throat. At first it was a monotone. One by one the Indians joined in. They accented their movements with a slight swaying as they worked over their weapons.

An Indian gave a sudden piercing, wolf-like howl. The others growled a response. The tempo quickened. Each Indian moved a little faster and began a definite stomping with the heels. After a long pause, there would be a thud of heels against log or ground.

A drum began to beat an urgent, staccato thump.

"They're sending the message." Squanto listened and then turned to Peter. Great amazement showed in his face. "What—what are they saying?" Peter felt hot all over.

"They say they are preparing for war, but not against Massasoit. They are going to fight your people, Peter. But, why? What has happened?"

Peter collapsed on a log with his head in his hands. He could never go back to Pawtuxet. He would be killed. All the colonists would be killed and it was all his fault for not being able to bear a little hunger.

He began to unfasten his blouse.

"Oh, Squanto, I'm the one who started it all. I'm the one who is to blame."

Peter's voice broke.

"You see, I brought this—this—" he could hardly get the word out, his throat was so dry, "this war challenge."

Peter unfastened his snakeskin and held it out.

Chapter Twelve

PLENTY TO EAT AT LAST

Squanto opened the snakeskin and poured out a handful of shot. He seemed speechless for a moment.

"Where did you get this? Do your people mean to make war on this tribe?"

Peter's eyes filled with tears. "Why, no. Of course not! I brought this as a gift for Chief Massasoit."

"You brought a war challenge as a gift? Massasoit is a friend to your people, not an enemy. Do you not remember the treaty made two moons ago?" Squanto's voice deepened in alarm.

"Yes, of course I remember, Squanto. I didn't know a snakeskin meant war. I knew it was important, and I wanted to give Chief Massasoit something valuable."

There was a flash of lightning. Thunder rumbled overhead. The Indians called to one another. The drum stopped, and as the storm continued, the Indians put away their bows and arrows.

Squanto talked to them and then beckoned to Peter.

"Your snakeskin has spoken the right language, Peter. They say the English speak in thunderbolts and lightning. They say English magic is strong. They will not make war on the Englishmen."

Peter sank down on a log again, this time because the relief was so great.

Rain pounded the earth. The Indians danced in joy, and the women ran to get containers to catch rainwater.

Squanto hurried Peter toward Pawtuxet.

"Oh, Squanto, this rain will save our corn crop." Peter ran to keep up with Squanto's long strides. "At harvesttime, we'll have a big feast of thanksgiving."

Squanto almost smiled as he pointed to Peter's bulging stomach. "Until then, no need to eat." Then his expression changed. He pushed Peter to the ground and put his fingers to his lips.

Two men came through the forest. Peter recognized the voices of Edward Winslow and Stephen Hopkins.

"Here I am," Peter called.

Edward Winslow and Stephen Hokins hugged Peter and scolded him at the same time. "What do you mean by frightening us so? Are you all right? Squanto, how does it happen that you are here?"

Peter told the whole story.

"So that's what happened. Well, we can't take you back now. You'll have to go with us, and Squanto too."

"Aren't we going back to Pawtuxet?"

"It's not Pawtuxet any more," Stephen Hopkins said. "Yesterday we voted to give our town an English name. The new name is Plymouth. Now we're on our way to see Chief Massasoit about our food supply."

"What gift are you taking?" Peter asked.

Stephen Hopkins unrolled a horseman's coat of red, trimmed with lace, and a copper chain to be used by Chief Massasoit's messengers.

"Let's be on our way," Edward Winslow urged. "We want to be there by nightfall."

Long before they reached Chief Massasoit's village, his people came out to greet them. Edward Winslow and Stephen Hopkins did not explain outright why they had come.

"Will the people of Chief Massasoit's tribe bring their furs to the English for trade?" Stephen Hopkins asked.

Chief Massasoit addressed his people. Squanto interpreted. "Am not I Massasoit, commander of the country around you? Is not this town mine, and the people of it? Will you not bring your skins to the English?"

All agreed.

Stephen Hopkins presented the red coat to Chief Massasoit. He was delighted and took off his fur cape, put the coat on, and walked up and down bending his arms and nodding with satisfaction.

That night Stephen Hopkins, Edward Winslow, and Peter were invited to spend the night in the chief's hut. The doorway was hung with beaver skins, and the roof sloped sharply. The heat was stifling.

Peter looked for the bed. He saw mat-covered planks raised about a foot from the ground. Chief Massasoit and his wife lay at one end. The chief motioned his guests to the other. Peter lay where the roof sloped lowest. When two warriors came in and squeezed themselves in the middle, Peter thought he could never bear lying in a cramped position all night. To make matters worse, something bit him on the leg. He wriggled and scratched.

"Be quiet, Peter," Edward Winslow whispered, and then he had to scratch too.

Peter felt more bites, and then he knew what was biting him—fleas.

Stephen Hopkins moved a little.

"Are the fleas biting you?" Peter asked.

"Yes, but lie still. We can't leave until daybreak. It would be an insult to Chief Massasoit."

The next morning Peter's eyelids were heavy from lack of sleep. He tried to keep awake while Edward Winslow and Stephen Hopkins explained the purpose of their visit to Chief Massasoit.

"Your tribe eats well," Winslow said.

When Squanto interpreted, Chief Massasoit bowed.

"We English are always glad to welcome the Indians as guests."

Chief Massasoit bowed again.

"But it is indeed a pity that we English do not have fine food to serve our guests. We regret that our food supply is so low that we cannot serve our guests as we would like."

With dignity, the chief stated, "Chief Massasoit will explain to his seven tribes that they must always bring food when they visit."

Edward Winslow and Stephen Hopkins bowed in their turn. As their parting gift, they hung a string of beads around the neck of Chief Massasoit's wife. She sucked in her breath to show her pleasure and fingered the bright-colored necklace.

Chief Massasoit's people ushered their guests to the

edge of the clearing. Peter waved good-by as he followed the men on the way to Plymouth.

The rain had saved the corn. A bountiful crop was in prospect as the harvesters began their work. Preparations for a big feast began.

Every day Peter had to bring back more buckets of water than the day before. Mrs. Brewster sent him to the stream so many times that he was tired out. He dawdled on the way by mid-afternoon, and just for fun, backed up Fort Hill while looking out over the harbor.

A young girl's voice broke into his thoughts. "Look sharp, Peter Cook. Mind the kettle. If it rolls downhill, you'll have to fetch it."

Peter's foot struck something hard. With a clatter the kettle bumped down the hill to the bottom.

"Have you lost your senses completely?" The girl scolded Peter but did not move from where she was sitting. Her thick green skirt spread in a circle around her. The breeze whipped a strand of her tawny hair across her mouth, and she flung it aside with impatience.

"Sarah Fuller, have you nothing else to do but sit halfway up and halfway down Fort Hill?" Peter sent a sidelong glance toward the kettle lying on its side at the bottom of the hill.

Sarah tucked her arms around her knees. "I've been helping mother mold candles since morning. I know we have enough candles for twenty years."

"But Sarah, weren't there other chores for you to do—such as pounding the corn for the pudding?"

Sarah made a face as she waved a hand toward the cornfield. "Think of all the corn puddings that field will make."

Peter groaned. "And think of all the shucking.

There'll be enough to fill the whole bay from here to—"

He jumped up. "Sarah, look! Do you see that speck way out there? It looks like a sailboat. But the shallop is anchored at the mouth of the river today."

They watched until they were sure it was a sailboat. They ran to tell the lookout.

Peter and Sarah ran to tell the people. One by one they left their work and gathered on the beach. It was the first ship the colonists had seen since they left England.

When the landing boats arrived, the first man to step ashore was Robert Cushman. The people of Plymouth greeted him with shouts and tears of joy.

"I've brought thirty-five new colonists."

Most of the newcomers were young men. They had not brought food, bedding, pots and pans, or extra clothes, but the good ship *Fortune* on which they sailed had brought a load of cloth. The colonists traded beaver and otter skins for it.

"Aren't you going to stay here with us?" the people asked Robert Cushman when he began to supervise the loading of the *Fortune* after a few days.

"No. I came over just to get the charter signed." He explained how the business difficulties with Mr. Weston would be solved as soon as the charter was signed. "Mr. Weston told me he intends to keep all his promises if you sign."

The vote was overwhelmingly in favor of signing. Robert Cushman sailed back to England with the charter.

All attention now centered on the harvest feast.

When the day arrived, Chief Massasoit came with ninety men. They brought five deer they had killed on

116

the way. While the women finished the food preparation and roasting of meat, the men had shooting contests with arrows and muskets. There were feats of wrestling and games of skill.

Peter and Sarah hung around the tables as the women brought the food. There were fish, venison, and wild turkeys stuffed with chestnuts. Hominy, corn pudding, and white bread were placed next to watercress, leeks, and grapes.

"There's enough food here to feed all of Chief Massasoit's seven tribes," Peter said.

When all had gathered at the tables, Governor Bradford gave the blessing.

"Heavenly Father, we are but pilgrims on this earth, and it is as pilgrims that we pause now to nourish our bodies that they may be fit instruments for thy work, that with renewed strength we may continue on a further pilgrimage to the heavenly city Thou hast prepared for us all. Amen."

With laughter, talking, and gestures, red men and white men sat down.

Peter unloosened his belt three notches and started to eat.

The Author

Louise A. Vernon was born in Coquille, Oregon. As children, her grandparents crossed the Great Plains in covered wagons. After graduating from Willamette University, she studied music and creative writing, which she taught in the San Jose public schools.

In her series of religious-heritage juveniles, Vernon re-creates for children events and figures from church history in Reformation times. She has traveled in England and Germany, researching firsthand the settings for her fictionalized real-life stories. In each book she places a child on the scene with the historical character and involves the child in an exciting plot. The National Association of Christian Schools honored *Ink on His Fingers* as one of the two best children's books with a Christian message released in 1972.